DIRTY DRAGON

A DRAGONS LOVE CURVES NOVEL

AIDY AWARD

Aidy Award/Coffee Break Publishing

www.coffeebreakpublishing.com

Publisher's Note: This is a work of fiction. Names, characters, places, and incidents are a product of the author's imagination. Locales and public names are sometimes used for atmospheric purposes. Any resemblance to actual people, living or dead, or to businesses, companies, events, institutions, or locales is completely coincidental.

Cover by Melody Simmons

Dirty Dragon/ Aidy Award. -- 1st ed.

ASIN B07Q85TCJ7

STRANGE MAGIC, A CURVY WITCH, AND A DIRTY DRAGON

Dax:

There's something strange in this neighborhood.

Who ya gonna call?

Dragon Warriors!

It will be a piece of cake to keep the Troika Wolf Pack pups and their adorably cute nanny safe from the non-existent threat.

The Black Dragon isn't interested in wolf cubs.

But I'm interested in sticking around to see if their nanny wants to have some fun. In my bed.

Jules:

Argh! The dragon warrior sent here to help me protect the pups is completely infuriating.

He's great with the kids (which I wouldn't have expected), and I want to kiss him until I can't see straight (which is completely distracting.)

But I keep having visions of a mysterious figure who is trying to change everyone's fate. She's very powerful and is blocking my second sight so I can't see enough to protect any of us.

Except when I'm with the dragon - then I see a future I'm even more scared of...

A very, very dirty future. Together.

Get down and dirty with this dragon tonight! Grab your book now.

This is a paranormal dragon shifter romance in the **Breath of Air Collection** and is a stand alone romance in the Dragons Love Curves series from bestselling author Aidy Award.

This one is dedicated to my peeps at Colorado Romance Writers! You all are the bomb-diggity.

and

Bill Jackson and his puppets.
Because...destiny.

ACKNOWLEDGMENTS

Oh how I lurrrve my Amazeballs! You all are the best reader group and street team ever! Thanks for always posting hilarious stuff to our group and talking books, boys, and body positivity with me every day.

Big sloppy kisses to Linda Dunn, Theresa Finn, and Corrine Akers for keeping us in smiles!

I write these books for you!

I've got special thanks to Crystal Albright, Jo-Anne Valcourt, and Telecia S.! Without you three the wolf pups would still be called Baby Girl and Baby Boy.

Mwah!

Super duper extra thanks to the magical new Just In Time Proofreading Team , Whose magic spells include the correction of commas, spotting of comma splices (obviously commas and I are not friends), and all-around good eyes!

Karen 'knows her commas' Kline,

Kat 'smarty-pants' Sarvis,

Kim 'killing it' McKinney,
Dawn 'dangerous' Combs,
Nicola 'notices it all' Summerson,
Jeanette 'maniac' Merrick,
Mary 'lovely lady' Lunsford,
Brittani 'bring it on' Jolley.
Krissie 'catches it all' Phillips.
Kim 'keeping it real' Devine,
Donise 'doing it right' Cinnamon
And Rachel 'ridiculously awesome' Dunlap

Thanks for making my butt look good.
Any remaining errors are all my fault.

Hugs,
   --A

Here there be dragons

—Really Old Maps

.

HELL'S BELLES

*I*f hell ever felt like it was freezing over, this was where it went to warm back up. Dax and his little band of Dragon Warriors, correction Demon Dragon Warriors, were hunkered down somewhere deep below the Burj Al Arab hotel in Dubai. The temperature above ground was a sweltering forty-five degrees Celsius. Down here at the entrance to hell it had to be twice that.

Dax reveled in the heat. Any Red Dragon Warrior loved a good hot, sweaty battle. Almost as much as he loved a good hot, sweaty battle between the sheets with a fiery redhead. In either, he had always won.

A flaming boulder whizzed toward them. Dax grabbed the warrior next to him and yanked him aside. It flew over their heads nearly missing taking the two of them with it. He whistled and patted the guy's shoulder. That was a close call and the perfect cue to get this mission underway.

"Ready to kick some ass, lads?" He looked each one of the dragons in his small band of newly deigned Demon Dragon

Warriors. They nodded to him in turn. Most Reds didn't want anything to do with these brand new additions to the AllWyr. Dax liked any man or beast who had the same fire in their blood and wanted to hunt demons and the Black Dragon to extinction.

Hatred for the bastards was seated deep in every Red Dragon Warrior's blood. Demon dragons, excuse him, demon wyrms could all suck it.

"We were born ready." Neo, the Demon Dragons' second in command was the last to meet Dax's challenge, but only because he'd been waiting for each of his brethren to agree.

Yeah, but they were also born yesterday, almost literally. If they weren't so enthusiastic about meting out revenge on the King of Hell, he'd be worried they weren't ready for battle. Jett, the Demon Dragon Wyvern, hadn't wanted any of them to risk their lives so soon after regaining their powers. Each and every one of them had volunteered for this mission. Dax gave Neo a salute of acknowledgment and indicated for him to present the plan.

"The intel we've brought you will take us directly into Geshtianna's hive. We'll go in here," he pointed to a crude map they'd drawn in the ash and dirt, "and you'll drive the main group straight through to the dungeon where the Golds are being held. Then we can chop the Succubus Queen into a thousand pieces and be done with her conniving."

See, smart and blood-thirsty through and through. Dax couldn't ask for a better command. Granted he hadn't asked to be in charge in the first place. He'd been the only one Cage, the AllWyvern, had been able to get to take this mission. Bring on the fire, bitches. He'd soak it up like sun on a tropical vacation. The Demon Dragons Warriors were right there with him, itching to get their hands around the necks of the demons they were related to.

"That's the plan, then. Everyone ready?" Dax knew they were, even if they didn't. Every dragon was born to destroy the minions of hell, even the ones who were born here themselves. These poor bastards wanted nothing more than to prove themselves in battle. They were going to get their chance tonight.

Dax gripped his sword and the others followed suit. Just in time, too, because the next wave of demon dragon wyrms poured in along with a barrage of fireballs. This was going to be fun.

His time hanging out with the Troika Wolf pack in America hadn't been wasted. Well, not all of it. There was that week when he and the strawberry blonde had whiled away the hours holed up in her cabin, naked. Good times, good times. Dax gripped his sword with both hands like a baseball bat. He pulled the hilt back all the way to his shoulder and then swung with all he was worth, keeping his eye directly on the fireball coming right for him. He connected straight on with his target and sent it hurtling back toward the oncoming horde with a little extra fire of his own to give it a bit of oomph. It hit the demon wyrm bastard right in the middle of the chest and it disintegrated into a pile of black oily goo and ash.

The demon dragons behind him watched and learned, turning the inner pits of hell into a fiery batting cage. He oughta start a team. Rah, rah, sis-boom-bah. Go Dragons.

It took them only minutes and a modicum of effort to destroy the first attack wave. It was if the forces of hell weren't even trying. The Demon Dragon Warriors hadn't batted an eye at taking out that horde. "I call that a home run. Now let's get those Golds and get them the hell out of hell."

Dax and Neo took point moving through the tunnels of stone and sand under the earth. He had to give it to these warriors. They knew how to move with some serious stealth. One minute they were behind him and the next they popped up in a shadow a few feet ahead to slash the head off a demon wyrm, or run one through before it even knew it was under attack.

Neo popped out of sight, took out a wrym above their heads, and then reappeared right in Dax's own shadow. Dax jumped about a foot and Neo laughed at him.

"Shit, you scared the Cheez Whiz out of me, you bastard. Don't be jumping in and out of my shadow, unless you're going to teach me how to do it too."

Neo grinned, which looked super weird and creepy on his normally angry face. "Us newbies gotta have some secrets to ourselves, Red. What is Cheez Whiz?"

"Only the greatest gift in all of snackdom. I'll buy you a bottle when we get back." Somebody had to teach these schmoes the finer points of the shitty human diet. No more blood and guts for their dinner. Unless steak counted. Mmm. Steak. Fine, Cheez Whiz and Ritz for an appetizer and then a steak dinner to celebrate their victory.

"Incoming." One of the warriors shouted from a few meters ahead and he wasn't kidding. The barrage of fireballs from a few minutes ago was nothing compared to the brim-stone raining down onto their position now. Not to mention the avalanche of sand and lava - make that glass shards and lava.

"Steady, warriors, steady. You know what to do. On my mark." Dax had expected resistance but these buggers wouldn't know what hit them when they saw the Demon Dragon Warriors transform into their dragon forms. It was going to be epic. Like Game of Thrones season seven episode four epic.

The first fireballs hit, but either smacked into the floor and walls were returned by the warriors. The river of lava crept closer and heat rose another billion degrees. Demons wyrms hopped around, flapping their useless little wings and squawking like the vultures they were. Three broke off from the main horde and aimed straight for the ready warriors.

"Now?" Someone down the line asked.

"Hold." They could not lose the element of surprise. The charging demons were almost close enough that he could smell their putrid rotten breath. Perfect. Dax counted down. "Three, two--"

He let the wave of hot magic he held in his soul wash over him and his dragon form burst forth. He lifted into the air and shouted into the warriors minds with his dragonvoice - *One. Go, go, go.*

The warriors shifted and one by one spread their wings, lifting up to the very top of the small cavern. As a single unit, Dax and the Demon Dragons opened their jaws and blew out streams of burning hot fire. The wyrms below flapped their wings trying to slow their forward momentum only to be toppled by the horde behind them. They charged head-first into the wall of deadly flames, frying in a second and disappearing into piles of ash.

Fuck, yeah. That ought to show any Red Warriors that the Demon Dragons were on the side of right. Dax flew in a wide circle, spewing fire down on any remaining stragglers that had escaped the onslaught. He brushed against something on the ceiling that was not natural. Rocks in this dry heat did not feel stringy or slimy. What the shit was up there?

Dax, look out!

Neo's words burst into his head and Dax took immediate evasive maneuvers. Whatever was on the ceiling was dropping down on top of them. Two of the nearest warriors to him were already caught in the net or web-like stuff.

"You dragons are so damn predictable." A male voice came from below and Dax caught a glimpse of a pale dude dressed in the worst version of a vampire costume he'd ever seen. Vampdickhead waved his arms and a succubus walked in, followed by about a dozen of her sisters, all escorted by an incubus of their own. The lot of them turned their lust magic on full blast.

Dax's body responded faster than if he'd been watching Triple X Red Heads on Pornhub. He lost his dragon form and crashed to the ground, landing flat on his face. At least he hadn't landed on his killer erection. He had his priorities to, uh, keep straight. Even in battle. His family jewels were safe, but the rest of his body was not, nor were the demon dragons.

The gooey web on the ceiling fell onto them ensnaring the entire unit of warriors. Some were still in dragon form and used their fire to burn the nets, but the goo must be some sort of magical protection. The nets didn't even singe much less burn away.

"Neo, I'm pinned down. Can you cut your way out?" Dax grunted with the effort of trying to roll onto his back and release a talon to shear a hole in the net. All the while, his body was on fire from the inside out with the force of the lust magic pouring through him. The second they got out of this mess he was finding a warm willing redhead to share his bed all night long.

"What the fuck is this stuff? I cut it and it grows right back together again." Neo's frustration was echoed by the other demon dragons fighting to get free.

"Well, well, well. I didn't expect to see a red-faced fool leading these demon bastards." The haughty voice of the succubus could be none other than their queen.

"I'd rather lead them than be shacking up with their dear old dad, like you, Geshtianna."

"I don't serve any dragon, black, red, blue, green, or even gold. Your AllWyvern knows that better than anyone. Didn't he tell you? The Gold Dragons serve me now."

"The hell they do." The dragon warriors served only their Wyvern and their mates. Not that Dax knew schmack about having a mate. Red Dragons hadn't figured out how to find theirs yet. "You might as well give yourself up now. We've got your number and Cage will be calling any second now."

"I don't think so. Because if he were to attack me, he'd only be hurting his precious dragons. Allow me to demonstrate." Geshtianna waved her hand and a line of Gold Dragon Warriors in their human form were led in. They had chains around their necks, dripping with the same goo as the nets and each were being wrangled by a succubus. Dax shivered, even with the heat of hell bearing down on him.

The warriors ' eyes were blank, and scratches made by fingernails, streaked their arms, backs, and even their faces. They shuffled with the weight of more chains around their ankles. The chains dripped with the goo, and something else. They were spelled with a very dark shining magic. These once proud warriors were indeed slaves.

Dax struggled to get free of the net again. "Cage is so going to fucking kill you in the face."

"Oh, yes. I'm sure. That's why he was too much of a coward

to come himself and had to send a little whelp like you." She turned her back on Dax, not worrying about him in the least. "You'll each have to double up, which will be a hardship for you, I'm sure. You may choose your new warrior slave in order of rank. Reversed.

The group of succubae murmured and grumbled, not liking that command at all.

Geshtianna could give a flying fuck. She was playing some card that Dax wasn't privy too. But leave these two for me."

She pointed to Dax and Neo. Fuck that. None of them were going to be turned into mindless fools. Dax would cut off his own dick before bowing to the likes of this evil bitch. He growled and called his dragon back up. Lust magic or not, these succubae were going down.

Gestianna looked down at Dax and licked her lips. "You're going to be a fun one. I can't wait to have you under me, begging for my bite." She hit him with a new round of her allure that made his head go fuzzy. His dick couldn't get any harder, but his balls drew up as if he was about to come like an untried teenager.

"Not. On. Your. Worthless. Life. Honey." He threw the cutesy nickname in there just so she knew that she might have him by the balls, but she didn't have his mind.

"You'll see." Another wave of her lust magic poured through him. Beads of sweat broke out on his forehead. Red Dragon Warriors didn't sweat. He blinked and gritted his teeth hard, fighting the lure of her power. "Feel that, whelp? We can do this the painful way or the pleasurable. It's entirely up to you. Well, not entirely. I do enjoy a bit of sadism with my tasty treats."

"Fuck." He breathed hard and forced the words to come out of his mouth. "You."

"Soon, pet. Soon." Geshtianna motioned toward the nearest succubus to come forward. The demon woman chose one of the Demon Dragon Warriors and made her slave pick the guy up off the floor and toss him over his shoulder. She clipped a spelled chain around the neck of the struggling warrior and he stilled, his eyes going blank as the Gold's eyes. Then they retreated into the nearest tunnel and into the blackness.

One by one, the women filed forward and chose their prizes, and Dax couldn't do a damn thing about it. Neo also continued to fight against his bonds and Dax even saw him try to flicker in and out of the shadow, but with no luck. Gestianna's hold on them was too much. Shit. There had to be a way out of this fucked up scene. Maybe if he pretended to give in, she'd release her hold on him a little and he could get the jump on her. Even the thought of pretending sexual attraction to this Bitchzilla was enough to send bile up the back of his throat.

What other choice did he have?

There were only two succubae left to choose. When the second-to-last made her choice and left the chamber, the last woman stepped out of the shadows. He instantly recognized her and her warrior slave. He was Zon, the captain of the elite guard of the Gold Dragon Wyr. She was the bitch who'd started this war in the first place.

"Come now, Portia. Don't leave your new slave waiting. I can't touch your rank, you worthless whore." Gestianna raked her nails over Zon's shoulder and fingered his chain. "But I can punish you by taking away your precious blood source."

Zon didn't flinch at the Succubus Queen's touch or threat, but Dax was sure he saw the warrior's eyes narrow just a little. Yes. Yes, he had seen it. Zon blinked, glanced over at

Dax and raised one eyebrow. It was a signal asking if Dax was ready.

"Do it," he grunted.

In one quick motion, Zon grabbed his own chain from Portia's hands and swung it up and over Geshtianna's head, encircling her neck as if she were Jabba the Hut. Her allure went from level eleventy-hundred to about a three just like that. Dax burst into his dragon form. He swiped the piece of gooey web from his back with his tail and threw it at the oncoming group of incubi who had been left behind.

Geshtianna grabbed at the chain and screeched, but Zon held it tight. "Go, brother. Tell Cage where we are and what we're fighting against. Now."

We're not leaving you and the others behind.

"I can't hold her off much longer and both Portia and I will be punished and put in isolation after this. Tell Cage to bring the mates. He'll understand."

Dax, we can not leave my brethren to be enslaved again. It will kill them. Neo had also gotten free with the use of his dragon form.

Portia stepped between the warriors and gave Geshtianna a death glare. "Zon. She's pushing back too hard. I can't block her much longer. We need to run now. I can't lose you too."

Zon nodded and his soul shard sparked. He gave the succubus another yank of the chain and let her drop to the floor. "Live to fight another day, Dragon Warriors. We'll do what we can to protect the new men as best as we can. I swear to you."

"Portia--" Geshtianna's strangled voice pierced the air with threat of death.

"Please. Go or we're all doomed." Portia fell to her knees and Geshtianna tore the chain from around her neck. Zon backhanded the Succubus Queen, sending her flailing halfway across the room. He scooped up Portia and held her in his arms like only a lover would.

We'll be back. I swear it. Dax shot a burst of flame at Geshtianna and the incubi under the net. *Neo, time to show me that shadow trick.*

Neo roared so hard and loud that sand and stone fell from the ceiling, but in the next breath Dax was surrounded in a cool blackness. The sensation of falling had him close to puking his guts out, even in dragon form. In the next breath he and Neo were back at the entrance to hell, in the underground parking garage of the Burj Al Arab.

Neo grabbed a silver Bentley Bentayga and threw it across the deck. The mangled body of the luxury SUV looked exactly like what Dax was going to look like when he reported what they'd found, and lost. He shifted back into his human form and his phone rang right away.

Yeah, of course it was Cage, the Alpha of all Dragonkind. It couldn't be anyone else. Fine. Great. Awesome. Dax answered.

"What happened down there, Daxton? You were just supposed to get some intel on this entrance into hell. Make us a God-damned map. Where is the rest of your unit?" Cage's voice came through at decibel level four-thousand and two.

Dax slumped against the nearest car. Cage had the best surveillance in the world so there was no doubt he was looking right at Dax and Neo. "I think it's safe to say, they're all now sex slaves and not in the fun way."

"Get up to the royal suite and give us a debriefing. Now." Dax shoved his phone back in his pocket and motioned for Neo to follow. He spent the ride up to the twenty-fifth floor trying to figure out how his mission had gone so wrong. When he got to the opulent suite that only a gold dragon could afford he was escorted into the hotel room's personal movie theater.

The screen was filled with hundreds of views of places all around the world, including the parking garage of the Burj, all projected by some state-of-the-art control center fully equipped with two tech covered warriors typing away on computers. This was how Cage knew about every single little thing going on in Dragonkind. He had a whole freaking spy network.

Hey. That screen showed the view from behind the Sleepy Folk bar the Troika Wolf Pack owned in Rogue, New York. He'd spent a lot of good times there making the moves on the ladies. That and watching baseball. But mostly the ladies.

"Daxton Cervony, Neo Nyuesi. Talk." Baseball and the ladies would have to wait. A good long time, if Cage's narrowed eyes, alpha voice, and use of their full names were any indication.

Dax spent the next hour alternating between dodging Cage's tiny tornadoes of rage and retelling him how their entire unit had gotten ambushed and the men they were trying to rescue had helped take the prisoners away. Neo didn't help one bit. He was just as flipped out as Cage.

"Cage, sir. Send us back in, give me some red dragons to demolish the whole place and we'll get those men back."

Cage stopped his pacing and wind whipping. He glanced over at his spy team and one handed him a tablet. He tapped at it and handed it back. "I know you would. We will be going back in, but you're going to the States."

Now was no the time to learn more about the fine art of apple pie. "Sir. I can do this. Don't take me out now because the last mission went FUBAR. I can--"

Cage held up his hand silencing Dax. "Gentlemen, I need

the room. Take five. There are steaks waiting for you up front."

Everyone but Neo immediately stood up and walked out of the theater. "You too, Demon Dragon. Dax and I need to work things out one on one."

Oh, shit. Dax knew he'd fucked the mission up, but was Cage going to murder him for it? No. Cage wasn't like that. Match, the Red Dragon Wyvern, might have eaten him alive, but Cage was cool. He hoped.

Neo shook his head like he thought Dax was dead, but apparently the promise of steak was too good to pass up. Dax hoped he was going to get one and not be served up as dinner.

"After today, I'm wary of giving you this mission. I need to know you can do what you're told and not go off trying to save the entire world. I get that you're anxious to turn any demon wyrm you find into a pile of ash, but we need some strategy to win this war, not just muscle. You hear me?" The full weight of Cage's alpha voice pressed down on Dax like an anvil filled with some real heavy shit.

Brains over brawn? Not exactly his strong suit. He'd always been the muscle. He should have known better than to try to lead a team nobody else wanted on a mission they weren't supposed to take on. Good thing he wasn't the alpha, or even the second in command. They'd all be demon dragon fodder. "Yes, sir."

"Good. Then listen close. I have another mission for you. This information stays in this room between the two of us. Do you understand, Daxton Cervony?"

Despite the pressure of Cage's expectations of obedience, and the alpha-command use of his full name, Dax stood up as straight as he could. He was a proud Red Dragon Warrior and would do everything in his power to redeem himself and save those dragons. "Yes, sir."

Cage stared him down, but Dax didn't break eye contact for a second. That must have been what Cage was testing because the tiniest of grins wiggled at the corner of his mouth and he leaned back against the desk. "Nikolai Troika contacted me through a private channel. One of his people is having visions of the Black Dragon."

"Okay?" That word came out sounding more like a question than anything else. What did that have to do with him?

Cage folded his arms and stared down at them. "They've requested assistance in investigating. We've already brought trouble to their area and I won't put their new wolf pups in danger because of our war."

Cage glanced at a framed picture sitting on one of the command desks of his mate, Azynsa the gorgeous mermaid, and their babies. Who looked a hell of a lot older than Dax remembered three-month olds to be. But what did he know about kids?

They had to be a motivating factor in sending dragons in to America. There were very few stationed there, but his old pal Steele from the Green Dragon Wyr was in the area. Somewhere along the coast, if Dax remembered right. Steele seemed like a better choice for this mission. He knew the wolves just as well. Better even than Dax. He'd mated a resident of the town who was friends with all the wolf alpha's mates.

No, Dax would better serve the war by staying here and digging out those tunnels and finding the demon wyrms. He would do his best to convince Cage that Steele could help the wolves out just fine and that he should stay. If Cage still insisted on sending him, he would go off on his own, and take out as many demons as he could. He'd seen which way the warriors had been taken. He could ferret them out.

"They've requested you specifically."

"What?" He had history with the wolves. Not always good.

"I was surprised, too. Steele will be available for backup, but I can't spare a whole lot of resources. I'm counting on you to figure out what's going on and if it poses a credible threat."

Shit. Guess he was going to America.

YOU ARE MY SUNSHINE

*J*ules hummed the last bar of the lullaby for the four-hundred and seventeenth time tonight. She didn't mind. If it helped the babies stay asleep, she'd sit here and quietly sing to them all night. She loved them both as if they were hers. They were as close as she'd ever have anyway.

Galyna whispered from the open doorway. "Jules, let them be and come have a glass of wine with me."

"Just a second. Tristan is going to wake up and if I'm here to give him his stuffed bear he won't wake Ellie.

Right on cue, Tristan rolled over, reached his hands up in the air and whimpered adorably. Jules placed the soft fluffy bear into his arms and he grasped it tight, burying his cheek against the fluffy tufts of fur. Ellie didn't even peek open an eye.

It's like you 're clairvoyant or something, Galyna gasped and threw her hands over her mouth and whispered through them. I'm so sorry. Ignore my stupid mouth. I didn't mean to bring that up. Sorry, sorry.

She wished the hair on the back of her neck didn't stand on end and her stomach would stop roiling with tsunamis of fear at the mere mention of that vision. Jules swallowed two or three times and then again. Everything was okay, there were no dragons trying to eat her from toes to nose. She was here in the nursery with a warm loving family who appreciated her. Everything was okay.

"It's fine, Gal." Her hands only shook a little when she pulled the cover up over the twins. "They should be good until morning."

Their mother crossed her arms and shot Jules a sidelong glance. "Good, because by then I can make Max get up with them. It's my turn to sleep in for once."

Jules knew she wasn't fooling anyone, but she appreciated how her friend pretended she had. It was silly of her to get so worked up about something that wasn't even real anyway. Still, if she never saw another dragon in her life, or her mind, she'd be happy enough.

Gal motioned Jules out of the nursery and into the cozy kitchen where two glasses of red wine were already poured. They moved to the living room, and Jules cupped her glass in her hands. She stretched her neck, rotating her head from side to side and then took a long swig of the fruity blend. "Ahh. That's the ticket."

The two of them settled into the plush couches. Gal tucked her feet underneath her in a move reminiscent of a dog curling up on a bed. Or rather a wolf. "They weren't too much of little monsters tonight, were they? I really appreciate you coming over on short notice to watch them. Again."

Shifter children were almost always little terrors, especially wolves. Throw in that these two were the children of the pack alpha and very few people in town wanted to babysit.

Jules didn't mind a bit. "They were fine. They only chewed through two blankets and six or seven stuffed animals before they wore themselves out."

"I should have stock in Build-A-Bear with as many of those things as we go through. Max thinks it's hilarious. I'm slightly horrified every time I find a stuffed animal's head ripped from its body and buried in the blankets in their crib."

Max walked into the great room and ran a hand along his wife's shoulder and followed his touch with a kiss to the same spot, right where her mark from him lie under her shirt. "They are wolves, my love. It's in their nature."

"I know. It's still strange to see Ellie carry her shredded bear around in her mouth like a fresh kill." Gal shivered. "It's going to be really strange when they shift in a few years and actually bring home what they hunt."

"You'll love every minute of it and be a very proud mama."

"Yeah, I will." Gal winked at Jules, her bubbly happiness overflowing in her eyes.

Jules wasn't jealous. Not even a little bit. Nope. Not her. "Okay, I should be going, I guess."

"Wait. I'm glad you're still here. Please, sit back down." Max held out his hand politely indicating the couch.

Jules knew better than to think that was a request. When the alpha of the Grimm pack asked you to sit, you sat. "Is there something wrong?"

"We all know there is. I know you'd rather ignore your vision, but I can't take that chance." Max perched himself on the edge of the couch, blocking Jules from going anywhere.

"I'm sure it's nothing. It hasn't happened again. Maybe I just dreamed it." Except dreams didn't usually happen in the waking hours. Nor did they leave a person with scars. Inside and out. She touched her neck where the last of the bite marks were healing.

"I can't take that chance. I've called in someone who I hope can help us. If what you saw was the Black Dragon, then we need reinforcements."

Gal put her hand over Jules's. She hadn't even realized she'd been picking at her cuticles until Gal stopped her. "We won't let anything happen to you. There's no way we can ignore a premonition like what you've had. Heli and Zara have taught us better. Please trust us."

Jules didn't have a choice. She wasn't anything special like the other seers in town. She didn't have special witchy powers over the elements, and she couldn't change herself into a beast. She was just a human. No one knew why the vision had come to her, only that what she'd seen was a warning of danger to them all.

"I do. You know I'll do whatever I can to keep those little ones safe." She almost added on that she loved them, but it would be weird because she wasn't even related to them. She was just their babysitter.

"Good. Our reinforcements will be here any minute. I'd like you to work closely with the warrior they've sent to understand what your vision meant and if he can help us fight and destroy any threat to my children."

"Our children, dear."

"Sorry, sweetheart. I get a little extra possessive of my family when someone tells me the King of Hell wants to kidnap them."

A flash of her vision popped into Jules's head. A huge black dragon had the babies clutched in its great claws and was giving them over to an evil shadowy figure in a dark cave while burning the city to the ground in its wake. She'd do anything to prevent that from happening. Anything.

A knock sounded on the door, three sharp raps that made her jump. God, she hated being scared all the time like this.

"That's him." Max got up to answer the door and she heard another deep male voice.

The Troika wolves had a lot of connections in this area and throughout the magical world. Whoever they called in to help could be anything from a mage to an alien bear-shifter star ranger for all she knew. She was hoping for someone more on the mage side. While she did trust the wolves in Rogue, New York, knowing that they had a beast hiding inside that could take over at any point still made her a little uneasy. At least none of them were dragons.

"Dax, you remember Galyna." Max escorted a supermodel, like underwear sports star cover of Men's Health and GQ hottie McHotsalot, into the room.

Wow. Had the temperature in here just gone up like a hundred and seventy-two degrees? If it wasn't completely embarrassing, she'd fan herself. As it was, she snuck her hands under the outside of her thighs to wipe any sweat off her palms. As if a super good-looking guy like this would even think twice about meeting her, but she didn't want to completely embarrass herself by making him shake a squashy hand when they were introduced.

"And this is our babysitter with the vision, Jules." The guy turned his dark eyes with the glow around the edges on her.

Gulp. Definitely a supernatural being of some sort. Maybe a god? The God of lust if her girly parts were any indication. Holy cow, she'd never had a reaction to a man like this in her life. "Hi."

At least she'd gotten that one word out. That was about all

her addled brain was capable of at the moment. It was a good thing Max had introduced her by name because she wasn't sure she knew what it was right about now.

"Well, hello there, Jules. It's very nice to meet you." Dax took her hand and kissed the back of it. Kissed. Her. Hand.

Swoon.

Or shock. Whew boy, when his lips touched her skin a surge of something like electricity but better shot through her. At the same time, the red crystal pendant he wore around his neck flashed and a red glow filled the room. He stared at her like she was both the love of his life and a threat to it.

"Who are you?" He clasped the pendant and shoved it inside of his shirt, blocking the light it was emitting.

Max answered for them both. "Jules, meet Daxton Cervony, the Red Dragon Warrior who is here to help us."

Dragon?

Shit, shit, shit. She yanked her hand out of his and took two giant leaps away from him. Her heart and lungs went into overdrive preparing her to either fight or flight far, far from the alluring danger of this predator who was ready to eat her.

Daxton held his hands out, fingers spread in a stance that was probably meant to show her he meant no harm. She wasn't buying it. "You, you stay away from me. And the children. I don't know how you talked your way in here, but you need to leave. Right now."

Max and Gal stared wide-eyed at her like she'd just told a little old lady to fuck off. "Jules. What are you doing? Dax is here to help. He's a Dragon Warrior."

Jules moved away again, sliding over the back of the couch to put it between her and the stupid dragon. "Like that's supposed to make me feel better. He's a dragon who knows Kung Fu, or Ninjitsu, or Ninjago. He's dangerous and either he leaves or I do. Didn't you see the way he was trying to hypnotize me or whatever? I'm telling you he isn't safe."

Dax tipped his head to the side acting all innocent. "Isn't Ninjago that Lego ninja cartoon? I hope I'm a better warrior than that."

"Don't you make jokes, you dinosaur in sheep's clothing."

He chuckled and man, it was a sensual sound. Dammit, why did evil villains have to be so damn hot? Spike, Loki, Gaston, the Joker, and now Dax. She needed to get her head examined. At least her body knew what it was doing. With every movement he made, she got further away from him and put lots of furniture blockades between the two of them. In fact, she was almost to the door and could make her escape.

Max turned into a blur and crossed the room, zipping up behind her and blocking her escape route. "Jules. This is not optional. I'm sorry if you are uncomfortable with the dragon. I swear on the moon in the sky, he will do no harm to you. If we knew of another way to find out how to keep the children safe, we wouldn't put you through this."

The bile rolling around in her stomach jumped up to the back of her throat. She swallowed and swallowed again, pushing her fear down as much as she could. It didn't want to go. "Fine. You want me to work with a dragon that I'm sure is going to kill me, I will. For Tristan and Ellie."

How the hell she was going to do it, without fainting dead away, was the question of the century. Ignore her fight or flight response? Yeah, right. What if she didn't have to be in the same room with him? All he needed was some information. He didn't actually need her. "I'm going home now and I'll call him, or better yet, text him. Then he can go off and do his dragony thing."

Up until that point, Dax had stayed where he was, which

was the only thing keeping her from pushing through Max's wall of muscles and out the door. Dax moved slowly around the blockade of furniture and toward her, speaking in a soothing lilt. "I understand you're scared, lass. I too swear, on the the First Dragon, that I will not harm you. I am only here to protect and serve. It will be hard to do that over the phone."

She wanted to believe him. She really did. Especially when he called her lass. Nobody had ever called her anything other than her name. The way he said that word made her think of illicit and naughty historical romance novels. Her mind and body were sending such mixed signals that she didn't know which way was up. Her head said run, her body said stay and never leave his side.

What the heck was wrong with her? If she got eaten or kidnapped and hidden away in some hoard of jewels and gold in a cave in the middle of nowhere she was going to... what? It's not like she had any supernatural powers except that one scary-ass vision of getting chomped on by a black dragon.

Regular old humans could become ghosts when they died horrific deaths, right? Good. "I don't like it, but I will work with you if I have to. But I'm telling you right now, if you murder me, I will haunt your ass until the end of time."

"My ass, huh?" He raised one eyebrow and damn it, there was definitely a spark of interest in his eye that made her want to curl up in his arms. He knew it too. "Could be fun."

Her fingers itched to flip him off. Which was one-hundred percent rude. If he really was here to help like he and Max promised, she could try to be a little bit nice. She clenched her hands into fists to keep them from running astray. "What do I have to do?"

Max and Galyna breathed a sigh of relief at the same time and then looked to Daxton. He'd continued to move closer to her and she hadn't even noticed his stealthiness. She'd have to keep a close eye on him. He'd need to earn her trust.

"First off, I'd like to know what you are. I'm guessing some sort of fire witch by the way you lit up my soul shard." He patted his chest. That crystal glowed brightly enough that the red light came through the dark black material of his shirt.

"I'm not doing that. I don't have any special powers. I'm nothing special. Just an ordinary human." She should change her name to Jane, because she was plain.

Dax came another step closer so that she had to tilt her head up to look at him. "You're definitely not ordinary. That I know for sure. You can reveal yourself to me. We will keep your secrets."

That sounded so dirty.

"No, really. I'm no--"

The world around her flashed into a cloud of TV static and smoke. Oh God. Not again.

The scream stuck in her throat and wouldn't come out no matter how hard she tried. She was sure she was pushing air and fear out of her lungs through her vocal cords but the world was silent, even if her throat did feel raw. If she couldn't scream, then she would run. But to where and what if she ran directly into the Black Dragon again?

"This isn't real, it isn't real. Get a hold of yourself, Jules. You are not going to die." It sure felt like it, though. There was something dark and evil in this hazy vision world with her. Its empty soullessness permeated her skin and pricked at her brain like a voodoo doll at an acupuncture convention.

If she could just pay attention this time maybe she could give Dax something better to go on than a big black dragon tried to eat me and kidnap the Grimm babies. Big breath in, long slow breath out. She blinked a few times for good measure and then stared into the static around her to see what she could find.

A shape was forming not too far in front of her. It started out small, about the size of a basketball, but with each passing second it grew bigger. Wait, it wasn't getting bigger, it was getting closer. Eek. If ever there was a time to run it was right now.

No. Breathe. It's just a vision. She could do this. Jules bit her lip to keep herself focused and from letting the silent scream building up inside of her from coming out. The blobby shape became three, two smaller ones moving along side a bigger one that took on some color. Red. Something huge and red was charging toward her.

Her legs bounced and wiggled of their own accord. They were going to run whether she told them to or not. Just a few more seconds and the red thing would come into view. Strange lightbulb-sized bursts of light popped up in front of the thing.

Uh-oh. Those weren't light bulbs. Those were bursts of flames. They shot through the static and straight for her. Right behind the balls of fire, a big red dragon flew out of the darkness and charged at her, spewing flames and death.

"Duck, dear." A beautiful lilting voice filled the strange space she was in, coming from no direction and every which way at the same time.

Jules got control of her body and spun around looking for her new ally. "Who said that?"

"If you don't drop to the the ground in the next half a second, your dragon is going to singe your hair. It's hard enough to shoot fireballs at the moving targets of those weird little Galla Demons that are after you without worrying about hitting your brown-dyed hair in the process. Do duck now or be prepared to spend quite a lot of time at the salon tomorrow. Although maybe you should make an appointment anyway and go back to your natural color. It suits you better."

The enormous red dragon opened its mouth and a long stream of fire shot right for her face. Jules did indeed duck. She covered her head with her arms and closed her eyes tight. The heat from the flames went right over the top of her head and the fast clickety-click of a clawed creature running past her filled her ears from both sides.

"Oi. Kids. I tell you. Such trouble makers." The woman's voice complained but she clearly thought whatever battle was happening over Jules head was more like a child's game of shenanigans. "You can wake up now, Jules. We'll see you again soon."

The voice had faded upon those final words and Jules had no idea if that promise was a lifeline or a threat.

DOOMED!

*I*f Dax had known that Cage was sending him to his doom, he still would have come to Rogue, New York. Because the end of his days had come in the form a gorgeous round-bottomed human babysitter with whom he was already a little bit in love. And she was scared to death of him.

She claimed she was human, but there was no way. She just didn't want to reveal her true self in front of him or the wolves. All the signs pointed to her being a fire witch. No other woman would have been able to light up his soul shard. Except his mate, of course.

She couldn't be that. Red Dragons didn't have mates. The Wyverns of the other Wyrs had started a chain reaction among their dragon warriors when they themselves had found their mates. Jakob, the Green Dragon Wyvern, started it all with his pretty mate and wife, Ciara. Then all of a sudden Green Dragon Warriors were finding mates all over the place. Like his friend Steele. Lucky bastard.

Steele's soul shard had lit up exactly like Dax's had when

he'd met his mate Fleur. Now they were blissfully mated and having more sex than wild rabbits. That was how, after hundreds of years, the dragon warriors figured out how to find their mates again. Reportedly with a little help from the First Dragon and the White Witch. Since then, the Blue Dragons, the Gold Dragons, and even the Black Demon Dragons had gotten their ability to find their mates back.

Not the Red Dragons. They had to wait for their Wyvern, Maciej Cervony, to find his mate before any of them could. But Match was off hunting some demon woman from hell who'd tried to kill him. So they had to wait. Which meant while Dax's soul shard had lit up exactly like Steele's, Jules was not his mate.

Fine by him. He didn't need a mate. He hadn't even hit his Prime years yet. He still had a lot of fooling around and one-night stands ahead of him before he was ready to settle down and be tied to one woman. He certainly wouldn't mind getting to know every inch and curve of Jules. His cock agreed.

First, he had to get her to trust him.

No, first he had to figure out what in the world was happening to her. A second ago, right when he thought he was close to getting her to take that first step toward trusting him, she'd gone all stiff and her eyes had rolled back in her head. That was weird enough. Galyna explained her body was in the grip of a vision.

That he could handle. What sent him into protection mode and brought his own dragon straight up to the surface were her screams.

She screamed so long and hard that within seconds she was going hoarse. Dax grabbed Jules to him, not knowing what else to do. He couldn't see, hear, or feel the danger she did. He tried to pick her up, but her body was like a stone pillar. All he could do was hold her in his arms until the vision passed. He didn't even know if she could hear him, but he talked to her anyway. He knew, from experience, that having a task or a mission in the face of fear dulled the anxiety to a manageable level. "It's okay, lass. We're here, you're safe. It's only a vision. Try your best to look around and see what it wants to show you so you can tell us when you get back."

She took a few deep breaths then and her body relaxed a little. Thank the First Dragon. Maybe she could hear him. Soft and soothing was not his forte. He was a warrior, not a nanny. He had the worst bedside manner and probably sounded ridiculous. He was much better in bed than on the side of it. If it helped her get through this vision, it didn't matter. "Good. That's it. I've got you."

He'd hold her as long as it took.

Maxsim was doing the same for his mate Galyna who looked like she was ready to climb the walls with her worry. "This is taking too long. She should be out of it by now. Something is wrong. Heli and Zara's visions only ever lasted a few seconds."

Dax didn't know anything about psychics but he agreed with Galyna when Jules's legs began to shake. "Is there any way we can pull her out?"

Galyna shook her head. "I don't know. I don't think so. I can call the girls to see if they know. What if she gets hurt again?"

Dax did not like the sound of that. "Hurt? I thought this was just a vision, how can she get hurt?"

"When she woke up from her other one, she had a bite mark on her neck and her arms had been clawed by something. She said it was a black dragon. She's only now healing because I had some of Fleur's magic dragon's breath balm."

A bite on her neck? By a dragon? Red fire swirled around the edges of Dax's vision.

It couldn't be. Was the Black Dragon trying to mark and claim Jules? Dax tipped his head to the side of Jules's neck and pushed her hair out of the way, dreading what he might see. If there was the black mark of a dragon there, he might just lose his cool.

He blew out a long breath he hadn't even realized he was holding when he saw nothing more than a bite mark. That was bad enough and he hated that she had to endure even the tiniest bit of pain from her vision. At least it wasn't the tattoo that came with being marked by a dragon. He couldn't imagine if anyone else's mark had been branded on her skin.

Not like he had a right to mark, claim, and mate her. But he didn't have to be happy about anyone else doing it either. Especially not something as evil as the Black Dragon.

Jules 's heart was beating so fast and hard he could feel it against his own chest. What the hell was happening in her vision? He'd always been happy with the amount of power he'd been given in life and his own dominion over fire, but right about now he sure as shit wished he was psychic in some shape or form. She gasped and then he wasn't sure if her knees gave out or she deliberately dropped to the floor, but within a second, they were both down on the ground. Jules curled her body into a tight ball and Dax did his best to encircle her with his own body.

"Shh, lass, shhh. Come back to us now. I'm here, I'll keep you safe, but you have to come back to us." She may want to haunt him if he killed her, but he would hunt down anything that actually hurt her, drown it in a river of fire and brimstone until it was so dead there was nothing left in this realm or the next.

"Red..." Jules eyes closed instead of being rolled back in her head and she mumbled. "Dragon. Red dragon."

Dax bowed his head slightly and found the crook of her neck with his lips. He pressed a small kiss there, ever so gently and slumped, letting the relief unlock his muscles. The vision appeared to be over now. He'd be perfectly happy if she never had another one ever again. That was progress if she was already asking for him. "I'm here, lass."

She snuggled into his arm, pressing her head against his shoulder. Her voice was quiet and sleepy, but not distressed any more. "Don't eat me."

He'd very much like to, but not in the way she meant at the moment. If she was his, he'd already have her-- better not to think about that right now. "I will make this promise as many times as you need to hear it. I will never harm you. You are mine to protect."

He hadn't meant to say that last part, but the words had rolled off his tongue anyway. To his own surprise, he did mean them. He'd never said the same about any other being in the world, much less an unclaimed woman. If any other dragons were around, they would be wondering if he'd found his mate.

Mates were the only women a dragon claimed like Dax just had. She wasn't his mate.

He didn't want one. He didn't need one. He couldn't even have one if he wanted a mate.

Not yet.

Her eyelids fluttered and her soft brown eyes stared up at him, all warm and trusting. "I am?"

He would protect her. Claim on her or not. Mate or not. "Yes, you are."

The tiniest of frowns turned the corners of her mouth

down and a vee creased her forehead as she considered his words. "Then why were you attacking me a minute ago?"

"Is that what you saw in your vision?" He hoped her visions were not predictions of the future. He couldn't imagine what would lead him to attack her. Unless she wasn't being truthful with him and was hiding her true self.

"A red dragon charged me, shooting flames. It was so angry and I couldn't get out of its way fast enough. I'm a bit surprised I'm not fried to a crispy crunchy crust."

Galyna crossed over and knelt beside them. "Did you see the babies again?"

Jules blinked a few times and her eyes brightened. She was rousing from her drowsiness. "I'm not sure. I was mostly concentrating on the dragon shooting fireballs at me. I think they might have been running alongside of it. But maybe it was wolves. I don't know. That doesn't make any sense."

Max and Galyna glanced at each other and he tipped his head toward another part of the house. Galyna hurried toward what Dax assumed must be the children's room.

A lot about this vision was bothering Dax. "Are you sure it was me attacking you?"

Jules swallowed, but met his eyes. "Are there other red dragons?"

She really was a newb to the supernatural world if she didn't know that. Maybe she was human after all. That didn't explain why his soul shard was practically burning a hole in his chest with the fire inside. "Lots. The Red Dragon Wyr is the oldest of the clans and the most umm, prolific."

He couldn't imagine any Red Dragon Warrior attacking a human, especially a soft, beautiful woman like Jules. Demon wyrms and evil black witches, sure, but not an innocent. Dax did not like the implications of that train of thought.

"Yikes." Her words portrayed worry, but her demeanor didn't anymore.

Nor did her scent. She smelled of peaches and warm cozy blankets in front of a crackling fire. If a dragon had attacked her in her vision, wouldn't she be more nervous about being around him? Something else must have happened in there too.

"You need not fear any of them." Would she believe that? She'd been off the charts terrified a few minutes ago. She had been trying very hard to get away from him, grasping at any method to avoid working with him. This could be a trick. Especially if she was a black witch.

"I know." As soon as the words popped out of her mouth, she tilted her head a wee bit to the side and her eyes flicked from side to side considering the validity of what she'd said. "Huh. Why aren't I afraid of you anymore?"

"You tell me." This woman was either very good at hiding her dark nature or the most fascinating creature he'd ever encountered. It made him want to stick around until the day Match did find a mate to see if she might be the one for him.

Wait. He did not just think that. No way. She might be dangerous. Either to all of mankind or maybe only his bachelorhood. Either way, he needed to be more careful of letting his libido drive his judgment of her.

"Magic?" she whispered all wide-eyed and expectant.

How was he supposed to answer that. Maybe she was trying to tell him something and wanted him to lead her into revealing her secrets to him. "Because you're a witch?"

"No." She narrowed her eyes. "Aren't dragons magic?"

Galyna came back into the room, a lot of the worry gone from her face. "The babies are still fast asleep. Their chubby little legs aren't running anywhere."

Jules sat up, propping herself on Dax's knee for just a moment before pushing off to stand up. "I'm so glad. I wish I understood better what was going on. I hate worrying everyone."

She wavered on her feet and Dax grabbed her by the elbow to steady her. No way that was feigned helplessness. He could not figure this chick out. "You're exhausted. You should rest. We can talk about this more in the morning."

Tonight he'd do some investigating on his own. It was either that or spend the night fantasizing about all the things he wanted to do to her body. Yes. He needed some space to clear his head. And a drink. He'd start his search for answers at the speakeasy owned by the Troikas. Plus free booze.

Plus other pretty girls that he could distract himself with.

So why didn't he actually want to go?

Maxsim glanced at him then at Jules and back. "Dax, will you escort Jules home?"

"I'll be fine, I don't need anyone to escort me. It's only a few blocks." She was already moving toward the door.

In a hurry much? Damn he was getting such fucking mixed signals from her. She was definitely hiding something. He should go home with her and check out her house, look for any indication that the demon wyrms had been there. Yes. He'd thoroughly search her kitchen, her living room, her bedroom.

Max folded his arms and puffed up his chest in that way all alphas did when they were ready to lay down the law. "I'd feel better if you allowed him to take you home. We don't know what this threat is or what it means, but we do know you're the key."

Jules clasped her coat to her chest and backed away. "I

don't want to be the key. I can't be. I'm no one special, you know that as well as I do."

She was about to go back to running scared. Dax wasn't going to get any information out of her if she did. Trust. She had trusted him for that brief minute after she'd woken up out of that vision and he'd held her in his arms. It faded as he questioned her.

Fine. No questions, more physical touch. Sounded like a good plan. Take her home, touch her.

No hardship there. He plucked her coat from her hands and held it out around her shoulders. "Don't worry about that now. Everyone is safe for the moment. Take the reprieve when it's offered."

Jules slid her arms into her jacket and Dax turned her to button it up. He leaned in close and whispered in his best seductive tone, "Let me take you home."

And do naughty things with you.

SHE WILL SURVIVE

A dragon wanted to take her home. A dragon.

What was worse was she wanted him to.

She really shouldn't allow it. Somehow she still found herself saying yes. "Okay. I guess that would be fine."

Fine? Really? When he'd whispered in her ear a second ago she'd felt anything but fine. Hot, achy, needy, wanting, wanton, but not effing fine.

She was going to blame her addled-headedness around this guy on that vision. This one had been very different from the last. At first she'd been afraid, she'd been petrified. She kept thinking how the Black Dragon was going to steal the children from her side.

But she'd survived. With the help of someone else. A woman. She simply could not get the image of anything besides that big red dragon and its fiery breath to form in her mind's eye. Whatever that woman had said changed everything. She'd taken the fear of all dragons away and replaced it with a calm trust.

That had to be a spell or something. All these stupid supernatural beings could take their transformations and their visions and shove it. Jules would not be manipulated, and she would not be afraid. Visions schmisions.

If she wanted to take a hot guy home with her, she was going to. Who cared if he could shift into a big red scaly beast the size of her teeny house. It was her choice to trust him. Not some faceless, nameless magical woman. Nobody was going to control her and her decisions.

But would she ever make the decision to take a strange man that she'd only just met home with her, after dark, with every intention to kiss him until she was weak in the knees?

Not yesterday. Not this morning. Not even an hour ago.

What had changed? Because she really wanted to grab Dax by the hand and drag him on out of the house, down the street and tangle tongues with him in the moonlight.

Maybe it was him. He was a flirt, that's for sure. She'd known other men exactly like that. They used their good looks and charm to get women to do exactly what they wanted. She'd fallen for it before.

She didn't feel like that's what he was doing, though. He was different. She couldn't put her finger on how, but his flirting didn't feel like insincere flattery. There was genuine interest in his eyes when he looked at her.

In fact, no one had ever looked at her the way he was right now. He'd waited for her to consent. He hadn't assumed she was going to say yes. That alone was enough to give him some of her trust.

She trusted him, but she didn't trust herself.

Had she ever?

Jiminy Crickets, she was overthinking this to death and

irritating even herself. Enough. Quit thinking and act. She grabbed Dax's hand and hauled him out the front door before anyone else, including the scared untrusting girl who lived inside her head, could say anything else. "Okay, bye. We'll see you all tomorrow."

Dax squeezed her hand and that gave her the smidgen of confidence that she needed to know she'd done the right thing. Probably. God, she hoped he wasn't going to get her home and murder her. She had threatened him with haunting if he did. So there was that. "I only live two blocks up and one block over. We can be there in a couple minutes."

The night air was still warm and a sliver of the moon hung low on the horizon. The slight haze from the humidity in the air made the stars sparkle and the whole scene was entirely too romantic. Best not to think of that and concentrate on getting home and figuring out what the hell she was going to do once she got there. One foot in front of the other directly down the sidewalk in the pretty suburban neighborhood. With her dragon in tow.

Jules dragged Dax a good block and a half, with only one more to go, before he slowed her down. "I love that you're in a hurry to get me home, lass. It's quite the turn on."

Uh-oh. His voice was a little too loud and a lot too creepy. Damn, she had made a mistake. Dax gently yanked her toward him and into his arms. She ducked her head to avoid his mouth coming down on hers, but he chased her and pressed his lips to her ears. "Pretend you're totally in to me and we're going to get down and dirty right here in the middle of the street."

Wait. Pretend? Jules heartbeat picked up and that old familiar tingle of fight or flight raced across the back of her neck. Her breath froze in her lungs. There was something out there and he knew it. But then Dax wrapped a big warm hand in the same exact spot and all of a sudden she could breathe again.

She leaned into his body and sighed, wrapped her arms around his neck and tilted her head to the side giving him more access to her neck and ears. "What's going on?"

"Don't be afraid. Well, do, but don't worry because I'm not going to let anything happen to you." He pulled her even tighter into his arms so that her body was completely flush with his. Her curves molded against his hard muscles, and there were oh so many of them.

Jules didn't have to pretend she wanted to make out with Dax. Not even a little teeny tiny bit. She pushed her hands into his hair and wrapped her calf around the back of his. "What am I not supposed to worry about?"

He brushed his lips along the skin at her neck and up to her ear. "Over there, in the shadow of the houses, there are at least a half dozen demon wyrms. They followed us from the Grimm house."

If he had said any other words she wouldn't have even cared. The sensations running up and down every nerve ending she had were on fire, burning for him. Their flames were stoked to burn even higher by the surge of adrenaline his revelation brought down on her. "We have to go back, warn them."

"I will. But first I want to get you safe. They're blocking the route to the turn I'm assuming we were to make up ahead because there are another six hiding under the various cars and in the bushes of the houses on the corner." Dax tilted his head to the side, indicating where she should look.

She didn't even know what she was looking for. Demon sounded bad, but what was wyrm? Demon worms didn't sound that bad, unless they were like the ones from the horror movies that dug up from the core of the earth to swallow whole cars and houses whole. Eek. Did the earth below them just tremor?

She held as still as possible so they didn't feel the vibrations from her body even though she was pretty sure she was shaking in her boots. "I don't see them. Or I mean, I guess I don't know what to look for. Which doesn't really matter because what are we going to do?"

"You aren't afraid of heights, are you?"

"No. Should I be?"

"As soon as they realize I see them, they'll attack. I can hold a dozen of them or so off myself, but where there's a dozen, there's more. If I can get you to safety I can call up any other dragons in the area and then come back and burn them all to the ground. To do that, I need to shift into my dragon form and fly you the hell out of here."

Big gulp. Like sixty-four ounce X-treme Double Big Gulp. "You want to turn into a dragon and I'm supposed to crawl up on your back and fly away?"

"More like you'll catch a ride in my claws. I promise I won't drop you. Ready?"

Oh, like right now? Crap. No. "Yes."

"That's my girl. Hold on." Dax kissed her then. Hard and fast and with a slip of the tongue. A brilliant red sparkle of light shimmered across his skin and in two blinks of her eyes she was looking into the snout of a fire-breathing dragon.

A red one that looked awfully familiar. Jules gaped at his beauty for a whole second before he blew a snuffle across her hair and lifted into the air.

Grab onto my leg and hold on tight, here they come.

Whoa. Mental telepathy. She was so going to ask him about that later. Jules jumped into the curled claw full of talons that he held out for her. It looked scary as hell but once she was wrapped up in his grasp, she felt safer than if she had a protective forcefield around her.

Good thing, too, because that's right when the velociraptors came out to play. If she had known that a demon dragon looked like an evil black dinosaur, crossed with a bat and an ostrich, with wings and beady red eyes, and also breathed fire, she would have been a whole lot more worried than she had been.

Dax's wings flapped in one great big whoosh and they gained fifty feet in altitude while the demon wyrms were blown back by the force of the blow. That didn't stop them, though. The second they recovered most of them took to the air as well and the chase was on. Holy crapballs was it on.

Jules hung on tight, but there was no way she was closing her eyes for a second. "Dax, look out. There's one on your three o'clock coming in fast."

Dax dove and spun just like a fancy jet fighter and Jules squealed. *Sorry, lass. I'll try not to do that again.*

"I loved it. Do it as much as you want. This is the best dragon fight I've ever been in."

A big rumbling sound came from the dragon's belly above her and she realized he was laughing. *Okay, then. Hold on tight.*

He wasn't kidding either. Jules gripped him with all her might and Dax dove and twirled and swirled, flying in and out and in between the demons in the sky with them. He shot great swaths of fire and caught several of the nasty little beasts in his flames. They flailed in the air and one burst into a pile of ash right in front of her face.

She continued to call out to him like a wing man when she saw the creeps trying to get into his blind spots. "One on your six and two more at four o'clock."

Next time they did this she was bringing a weapon, a shotgun, or a rifle, or a slingshot at least, so she could help too. No way these bastards were getting anywhere near those sweet babies if she could help it at all. She knew Dax's original plan was to get her out of there, but they were working well as a team and the demons ' numbers were dropping like flies as he eviscerated one after another.

We've almost got them. Can you hang on a little bit longer?

"Yes. Get them, murder their asses all the way back to hell."

Yes, my blood-thirsty lassie. Dax beat his wings hard again like before and pulled up into a wide arcing backflip, swooping over the heads of the group on his tail, and coming out behind them. He spit out a series of rapid release balls of fire and took the whole clump of demons out bang, bang, bang.

When the last one exploded into flames and oily black demon bits rained down on the street below them, she let go of Dax's leg for one brief moment to thrust her arms in the air in a double fist pump. "Yeah. Take that, you suckers."

In the middle of her victory cheer something that smelled like the rotting carcass of a skunk high on stinkweed grabbed her arms with razor-sharp talons and yanked her out of Dax's grasp.

Her stomach leaped up into her throat, presumably trying to stay in its rightful place in the safety of her dragon's claws. She fell at least ten feet full on thinking she was going to die splattered along with the ashy remains of the enemy in the middle of Elm street. The demon wyrm was grabbing at her legs and arms but all it managed to do was cut and scratch her.

Hold on, Jules. I'm coming. His voice in her head was cool, calm, and collected, like free diving to her death was no big deal. His confidence that he could save her helped, and the next time the demon dragon grasped at her she punched it in the face. "Ow."

Dax cut the damn thing all the way in half with one of his talons and scooped her into the other one about three feet from the ground. Jules hadn't even noticed she was that close yet because she was concentrating on the other thing trying to kill her. They glided back down the block to the Grimm house and Dax set her gently down in the grass in the front lawn.

The outer motion detector lights were already on as Jules dashed up to the front door. She had to warn Max and Galyna as soon as possible and make sure the babies were okay. She wanted to check on them herself, see their cherubic little faces, and give them a kiss.

If that's what was after them, they were not only going to need backup from Dax and any other dragons he could round up, but the rest of the packs in Rogue. Max as the alpha of Grimm could contact his brothers and sound the alarm.

Jules, stop. Look. The front door is open, but the house is dark. I can smell the taint of the wyrms. Do not go in there. It isn't safe.

No. Oh no, no, no. She ignored Dax's command and burst into the house. The furniture was in shreds, anything not nailed down was askew and none of the family was in sight. What if they were dead? What if the babies had been kidnapped like she'd seen in her vision. "Gal? Max?"

An arm came around her from behind and pulled her back into the darkness of the foyer's coat closet. She opened her mouth to scream but a hand slapped over her mouth. "Lass, shh. It's just me."

She nodded and he removed his hand. "We have to find them. Right now."

"It's okay, they're here and they are okay. I caught their scent along with the demon wyrms. If they are hiding, we don't want to out them. Understand?"

"Yes. But what if they are hurt? Please help me find them. We have to help protect those babies. I know that's why I was sent that vision."

"It might be." He let her go and stepped to the front of the closet and looked both ways. "Take my hand and no matter what, do not let go. They are toward the back of the house. I will lead you there. You keep an eye out behind us just like you did when we were in flight. I can destroy demon wyrms in my human form too, but it's a harder fought battle, so a lot of warning if we're under attack will be good."

"Got it. Let's go."

They stepped back into the foyer and this time Jules took in a whole lot more than the overturned furniture. There were giant claw marks in the carpet and along the walls. Demon's or wolf's? She couldn't tell. They crept into the hall and toward the nursery. The door was closed, but there were giant basketball-sized holes that went all the way through it.

"This is where their scent is the strongest. Softly call to them, so we don't startle them with our approach. They'll be in beast form and ready to strike out at anything that could be a threat, including you and me."

"Okay." Jules swallowed and put her mouth near one of the holes in the door. "Gal? Maxsim? It's okay, Dax and I are here. We killed a bunch of demon things outside."

Nothing.

"Are you in there? Are you injured? Can we come in and help?"

This time a very low and dark growl came from inside the room. Then another joined it. That had to be Max and Galyna in their wolf forms. A second later a tiny little howl resonated through the air, follow by another slightly higher pitched one. Uh. That wasn't either of her friends? It sounded like wolf pups howling at the moon. But the babies weren't old enough to shift. They wouldn't learn how to become wolves until they were around five years old, according to Selena, the matriarch of the Rogue pack.

Jules carefully turned the knob on the door and pushed it open. The growling increased, but this time, it was followed by little yips and yowls.

"It's just me. I'm going to come in, very slowly, and I'm bringing Dax. Don't anyone attack us, okay?"

"This isn't a good idea."

"I have to make sure the babies aren't hurt. There's something weird going on." Jules slowly peeled herself off the wall and stepped into the doorway to the room. It was darker in here than the rest of the house and it took a second for her eyes to adjust. The first thing she saw were the glowing icy blue eyes of Max's giant wolf crouched in front of the crib the babies shared.

Galyna's wolf sniffed the air and then nosed Max. She sat down on her haunches and turned her head back toward the crib, too. Up over the side railing popped two fluffy little heads of the cutest wolf puppies in the whole wide world.

"Tristan? Ellie?" At their names they lifted their noses to the sky and yip, yip howled. When their adorable wolf song was done, one of the two sneezed and a toddler with the same blue eyes and blond hair as Tristan sat in the crib in its place.

The other wolf pup wagged its tail, licked his face and jumped on him.

"Ellie, stop. Gwoss. Quit it."

The other pup stretched and shook her head and sneezed. In its place sat Ellie, but definitely not a baby either. "Hi, Juwels."

ANKLE-BITERS

*H*oly First Dragon, Dax was never ever having kids. They were cute and all, but also these ankle biters were literally biting his ankles. He picked up one wolf puppy in one arm and yanked the other one off his pant leg and tucked it under his other arm. They wriggled and whimpered and yipped in protest at having to stop their brand new favorite game of chew on Uncle Dax.

Jules took one of them from him and ruffled its head. Galyna took the other and cradled it in her arms exactly like a baby. These little terrors were no babies. At a sneeze or a tickle or even if someone said their name they shifted between forms. Little kid, wolf, little kid, wolf.

"I don't like this one bit. When I find out what kind of magic robbed me of watching my children grow up and learn to walk I'm going to--"

Galyna set one wolf pup down, who immediately came over and started chewing on Dax's jeans again and took the other one from Jules. "What, babe? Forbid it? You don't know that it wasn't the response to extreme danger that caused this little insta growth spurt and their ability to shift to come on. Grab Tristan. Poor Dax isn't going to have any pants left in a minute."

Max was spitting mad, but there was also a glow of pride about him every time he saw one of his kiddos turn into a wolf. He scooped the puppy up who shifted in mid-lift and giggled when his father tossed him into the air. "Maybe. But I reserve the right to kill something. Besides, my mother will chew up and spit out the entrails of any being that interfered with her plans to film every second of her grandchildren 's lives from first steps to first shift and put it on WolfSpace."

Galyna cooed and tickled her wolf pup's belly. "Yes, that's right. Grandma is going to eat their entrails. Yes, she is."

Dax had already failed in the duty Cage had given him. He was here not even an hour and he'd allowed demon dragon wyrms to invade the Grimm home. Because he'd been distracted by Jules and her luscious body. He only considered for a second that she had purposely created the distraction. When she warned him of the wyrm on his tail and then worked so well with him in battle it was almost like she was a trained warrior who didn't have the ability to shift. She hadn't fought, but she had been an excellent navigator and kept a cool head in a crisis.

He knew seasoned warriors who would have flipped their shit in a free fall toward the ground. She'd punched the demon in the face and gracefully waited for him to grab her out of the air. So fucking hot.

He'd almost lost his own shit when she'd been snatched out of his claws. He swore that some divine gift from the First Dragon had given him a burst of speed and power to get to her on time. He'd never flown so fast in his life. He also knew in that last split second that if he didn't save her and she died, he would burn down the world.

She had to be his mate. He knew he didn't get one yet, that he had to wait for Match to find his first. Wait he would. The second he was able to give her his soul shard he was going to. She was the one.

Dax knew more than one dragon who'd gone a bit mad in the head thinking he would never find the one. None of their fathers had. It was a wonder any of them had been born at all. Well, except dragon warriors were the horniest bunch of beasts on the face of the planet. Sex brought babies. Mates brought love and babies, as now proven by the AllWyvern Cage and his mate, Azy. Their children had been stalked by the Black Witch even before birth.

The Black Witch. She'd tried to kidnap the dragon babies too. "Max, Gal, I'd like to bring in some more dragons and set up a protective detail for your children. I don't understand why or how, but I think the Black Witch may be trying to kidnap them."

Jules shifted on her feet. "But I saw a black dragon trying to take them, not a witch."

Dax would need to remain vigilant over his emotions and his damn libido around Jules until this problem resolved. She could so easily distract him and he had some proving of himself to do. After that, all bets, and all clothes were off. He crossed his arms and blocked those last thoughts down. "Ereshkigal has many skills. Possibly that's what she wanted you to see to throw us off the scent. But she tried to steal Izzy and Apollo before they were even born. She couldn't get to them and I think now she's after your pups."

Max's wolf shimmered up to the surface, making his eyes glow. "What the hell do we have to do with the dragons' battle?"

"I don't know. But I will find out." First he needed to get in touch with Cage and check his theory out and call for some reinforcements. This was not a one-warrior job.

"Fucking dragons," Max growled.

Tristan clapped and giggled. "Fucking dwagons. Grrr."

The adults in the room all went wide-eyed and Galyna gave Max a hard stare. He shrugged. "Kid's not wrong."

Jules was doing her best to hide a smirk. "Guess we have to start watching what we say around them. It's incredible how they not only grew, but their mental development seems to be right in line with how old they appear to be. Like maybe around three-ish?"

"Did I just hear my grandson swear?" Selena the Troika matriarch picked her way into the disaster of a living room. "The other boys and their mates are on their way over, too. I see we'll need to call in more to get your place back into livable order."

She walked right up to her son, Max, looked at the child he was holding and held her arms out for him. "Aren't you a big boy now? Come here and tell Babi what you've been doing to get so big."

Two seconds later the alphas of the other two packs in town, and Max's brothers walked into the room with their mates. "Holy shit, dude. What the--"

Max slapped a hand over his younger brother's mouth. "For the love of the moon, don't swear in front of the kids. I've already made that mistake."

The women rushed over to Gal and Selena and the five of them turned into a storm of gestures and talking over each other and laughs and gasps. His Jules was right there in the middle of it all holding her own with the alpha women of entire wolf-shifter world. She glanced over at Dax and gave him a soft smile.

Dax never intended to stay in America long term. This place was always just his favorite R and R spot. He figured he'd get stationed somewhere warm and tropical. He hated the cold. All Red Dragons did. He'd suffered enough brutal winters in Poland where Match the Red Wyr had decided to keep the Wyr. He supposed he could handle a New York winter.

"We've decided we should put the nursery back together first so the babies, uh children, can go down. They're already looking sleepy and I don't want crying, angry toddlers on my hands tonight." Galyna patted the back of the little girl who'd finally shifted back into her human form and had her thumb in her mouth.

"Here, give her to me. I'll watch them while you get the room how you want it." Jules took the child and the little girl curled into her shoulder, laying her head on Jules like the comfiest of pillows. She was fast asleep in seconds.

Tristan held out his arms toward Dax, opening and closing his hands in a gimme motion. "Fucking dwagon, papa."

Maxim chuckled and shrugged at Dax. "You wanna take him for a minute? The rearranging of the nursery will go faster if the three of us help. He jerked his thumb at his brothers. "We 'll be finished in no time and this little guy will probably already be asleep by then."

"Sure. If you trust me."

Maxim handed Tristan over who bounced in Dax 's arm. "I don't, but I do trust Jules. She 'll keep you in line."

All three men gave Dax either a slap on the back or a sock

in the arm as they filed past Dax and down the hall toward the nursery. He deserved it. No way was he letting any demon wyrms harm anyone in this family again.

Man, Jules looked so right holding a small fry in her arms. Something warm bloomed behind Dax 's heart. He rubbed the spot with his knuckles. Probably heartburn.

He really needed to walk outside and make a call. He didn't want to worry the wolves and Jules more than he had to, especially when he was still the lone dragon warrior. He 'd go call Cage and Steele in a minute. That little girl had to be getting heavy and Jules needed someplace to sit.

Dax cradled Tristan in the crook of one arm and grabbed the corner of the couch with the other. With a flick of his wrist he flipped it upright and waved Jules over to sit. There were claw marks like open wounds in the material, but it wasn't that much worse than the furniture in Dax 's own place. He hated to spend any of his growing hoard on stuff like that. He did have a pair of gold and ruby earrings that would look great on Jules.

She laid Ellie in the corner of couch and reached for Tristan who had indeed fallen asleep in Dax 's arm. She nestled them together and then propped pillows in a makeshift fort all the way around them. The children fussed for a second and Dax held his breath, hoping they weren't about to wake up and start screaming their heads off. Jules reached into their little nest and laid one of each of their arms over the other one until they were embracing.

Silence.

Dax whispered. "You're really good with them."

"I love them as if they were my own. I don 't know why, but I feel a very special connection to them." The children felt it too. No doubt. There was something special about Jules, human or not.

Huh. Did everyone feel drawn to her too? Was he kidding himself thinking his attraction to her was special? She did live in a town where all magical beings were welcome. Maybe someone had bespelled her. Didn't sound like something the Black Witch would do, as conniving as she was. No, attraction, especially like what he was experiencing, was more likely the work of a succubus. It wouldn't be the first time a dragon warrior had been tricked by one.

Once again Dax warned himself to be careful around her. Once he was out of sight of Jules, he would examine these intense feelings he was having and ignore the signal his soul shard was emitting. If this was a spell, it was well hidden and very crafty. She claimed to be nothing more than human and he couldn't scent anything different than that on her. If her story checked out he would keep her close and protect her from whatever dark forces were trying to use her against the wolves and dragons.

Jules yawned and Dax wrapped his arms around the back of the couch, urging her to lay her head on his shoulder. "It's late and you've had a very adventurous night. Sleep for a bit. I'll watch the kidlets. They can't get into much trouble if they're asleep."

"I am pretty exhausted. I'm not much of a night owl." She curled into him and within a few seconds she was softly snoring.

Adorable. She fit perfectly against him, her soft curves against his hard... uh, everything. Some parts of him were getting harder at the moment. Down, boy. Maybe later. Hopefully.

Jules felt so nice and warm in his arms that his own eyelids drooped a little. She wasn't the only one who had a killer day. He'd flown halfway across the world to meet her. Okay, not only to meet her, but she was a big part of this mission. One that he'd do anything to protect and keep safe. Along with those cute AF kids.

Dax stretched his neck muscles with a side to side movement of his head, trying not to disturb Jules, and yawned. He caught a faint whiff of something smoky before laying his head back on the couch and closing his eyes.

The first thing he saw in his dream was Jules, running through a field of daisies in the sunlight toward him. The rays glinted off of her hair, highlighting red strands that he wanted to reach out and touch. She was shouting something he couldn't quite hear. He reached out to catch her and wrap her up in his arms. That's when he saw the fear on her face and the sound of his name being yelled popped into his consciousness.

"Dax, Daxton. Wake up, you fucking dragon." Maxim shook his shoulder and his arm was pulled back and his hand was open, poised and ready to slap him across the face. "Where the fuck are my kids?"

"Krphs frrr nurrph thurrr." Dax's mouth wasn't working right. He blinked and even that small movement was slow and labored. "Wha wrong wuff me?"

Galyna grabbed Jules and shook her. Her only reaction was for her head to fall to the side. "Oh my god, oh my god. Someone has poisoned them and taken the babies."

The rest of the family were standing in a semi-circle in front of him and Jules. All were glaring at him. Which if his brain would work for a second, he knew was appropriate. All he had to do was watch one woman and two sleeping children for like five minutes and he hadn't been able to do it.

If there was a way to resign from being a Dragon Warrior he would do it right now. That was not an option. He shook his head, trying to brush away the cobwebs of whatever the fuck was wrong with him. "Dragons aren't affected by drugs."

There. An entire complete sentence. That was a start. "Help me up. I'll find whoever did this."

Maxsim reached for Dax's collar, ready to heave him up off the couch, but stopped short. Jules's body tremored, and then shook, and then she went into a full-on seizure. That did more to clear Dax's head than anything else. He welcomed the adrenaline that pushed through his veins and arteries restarting his heart, lungs and brain.

Dax scooted to the side and laid Jules out on the couch. He fell to his knees onto the ground beside her and pulled Jules to her side to help keep her airway clear. The soft pillows of the couch helped protect her head and all they could do was wait. "I think she's trying to pull herself out of it."

The jerky motions of her body slowed and Dax carefully stroked her hair. She took one giant gasp and her eyes popped open. "She took them."

"Who?" Galyna was wrapped in a giant group hug made up of all the other women in the room. They all were practically holding their breaths waiting for her answer.

Jules blinked again. "I don't know. I couldn't see anything more than that. She filled the room with some sort of smoke or fog or light. It was almost like a laser show behind my eyelids. Then she called the children and they shifted and ran outside."

Max growled and fell to the ground on all fours. His face elongated and fur erupted all over his body. His clothes exploded off his new wolf frame and in an instant he was sniffing the ground and took off running out the front door. Kosta, Niko, and Selena followed.

"They'll find them, Gal. There are no better noses on the ground than the alphas. If the children are in their wolf forms and running, they won't get far." Heli stared out the front door, her wolf eyes glowing. All three of the women's wolves were also close to the surface.

"We should stay here in case they come back. I'm going to get Jules some water. Dax, you should come to the kitchen and help me do that." There was a bit of alpha in Zara's request. She was the Tzarina of all of wolf kind and was used to having her orders followed.

"I'll be right back, Jules." Dax got up, wobbled a bit and then went into the kitchen. It wasn't far off the living room and he could hear Zara opening and closing cupboards. When he turned the corner he didn't see any glassware or pitchers of water on the counter.

"You listen to me, dragon." She pointed her finger at him. "You call in all your friends and you find those kids. Then you get this dragon problem out of my lands. You may have helped create our pack's bond with the dragons all those years ago, and I will never forget the service you did for me and Niko. If anything happens to those kids or anyone else in Rogue and the pack territories, that will be the end of wolf and dragon relations. Forever."

Well, shit. Not only was Cage going to kill him for doing a piss poor job on this mission, he was also going to extra super-duper kill him for creating a rift between two of the most powerful supernatural species in the world. Add diplomacy and negotiating a peace treaty to his to do list. "I hear you, my lady. I vow I will find them. I'm sorry your family has been made to suffer."

Zara folded her arms and her glare was extra powerful with the blue glow of her wolf in her eyes. "You do that. Then you're out of here and I don't ever want to see you in pack lands again. Do I make myself clear?"

There went his plan for spending the cold New York winter in Jules's bed. "Yes, my lady."

WHICH WITCH?

*O*h no. Oh no no no no no.

    The children were missing, probably kidnapped by some evil monster and it was Jules's fault. Damn these visions. Why couldn't she have been born with real supernatural powers and not a stupid plain human? Sure she'd dabbled in some elemental witchcraft. There wasn't a teenager in all of Rogue who hadn't. Didn't matter if they were human or special, everyone tried it. She'd even convinced herself that she'd turned rainy weather into a bright sunshiny day for a picnic with her friends once.

Of course she was kidding herself. The only time she'd ever come close to being a part of the real supernatural world was at last year's all-pack mating ceremony. The Troikas and the people in Rogue were the only family she'd ever really known. She'd hoped that one of the wolves would choose her for a mate. She didn't care which pack he was from, just as long as he wanted her and she got the chance to go through the change like Galyna, Heli, and Zara had.

It hadn't happened. Not a single wolf had even sniffed her

way. She wanted to be disappointed. Somehow, she wasn't. The Troikas still welcomed her into their lives. Not for long if she didn't get her rear in gear and figure out how to find and keep those children safe. Maybe Heli or Zara could help her figure out how to control her visions, use them instead of the visions using her.

That's what it felt like. It was as if some outside power was pushing into her head and forcing her to see and experience the darker side of the world.

Except for Dax. She'd been afraid of him both when she met him in person and in her vision. She'd been wrong about him both times. A strange connection to him pulled the fear out of her and replaced it with something in between comfort and excitement.

That sounded stupid even to her, but that's what it was. She'd never been so alive as when they'd been flying through the air fighting demons together. She also knew that when she laid her head on his shoulder and closed her eyes, he wouldn't let anything bad happen to her. Weird since she'd only known him a couple of hours.

The desire to keep him safe whipped through her like a warm spring zephyr. They were both in a lot of trouble now, even though everyone knew it wasn't really their fault. Dax had told her to stay put when Zara called him into the kitchen. Lame. Either the Tzarina was going to give him useful information or murder him with cookies.

Zara's icy voice floated to Jules's ears before she made it into the kitchen. "Then you're out of here and I don't ever want to see you in pack lands again. Do I make myself clear?"

Uh-oh. Jules didn't like the thought of Dax being forced to leave. Nope. Not at all. She didn't know why, but he needed to stay in Rogue. Like a really long time. Like forever.

"Yes, my lady." Dax sounded suitably chastised but still respectful and not like he was kowtowing to Zara.

Jules understood all the wolves anger, but she wouldn't stand for it to be directed at Dax when he'd done nothing but work to protect them all. She rounded the corner into the kitchen, put her hands on her hips in her best Wonder Woman power pose and looked Zara dead in the eye. "No. Don't go blaming Dax for any of this and thinking you can kick him out. He's already protected us all from super creepy demon lizard men and was knocked out by some kind of drug or spell for his trouble. Who knows what might have happened if he hadn't been here."

Zara raised her finger to halt Jules's speech, but there was no stopping her now. "I know you're the Tzarina and what you say goes, but your anger is misdirected and I'm here to tell you it will do more harm than good to make Dax the bad guy when we all know he's the one who is going to help us save the kids and defeat this threat.

Jules had seen any and all of the women here tonight shift into their wolf forms before. It was a common occurrence in Rogue. So she recognized the signs of Zara's wolf being close to the surface and ready to lash out at her. She had come off a little strong, telling the most powerful woman she knew to shove off, but she wasn't wrong and if ever she was going to prove she was worthy of being more than just a human, it was now.

She lifted her chin and held her arms straight at her side. It took all her confidence to maintain eye contact with Zara's wolf. They were officially in a stare-down.

Uncomfortable.

Zara relented first, narrowing her eyes and then glancing between Dax and Jules. "You're right, Jules. I apologize. I can't say I'm not still mad at your dragon, so I'm telling you now, it would go a long way if you two were to go find those babes."

Your dragon. Someone else had said that to her recently. She couldn't quite get a grasp on who, though. Seemed silly, he wasn't hers at all. He was a sexy wild thing and shouldn't ever be tied down.

Well. Except maybe in bed.

Jules 's eyes went wide and she had to keep herself from gasping out loud. She had not just thought that. Not once in her entire life had she even considered something so dirty. Zara was a known clairvoyant and Dax had spoken into her mind earlier. She was going to die if either of them heard what had just gone on in her mind.

Neither of them even flinched. Wait. Did Dax have a new sparkle to his eye? No. That must just be the lights in the kitchen. Okay, phew. No one, especially Hotty McHottsalot needed to know her mind was in the gutter when there were way more important things to be worried about. Jules pulled her mind back up into the light and cleared her throat. "I'm ready to do anything I can to help find the children. I wanted to ask you, Zara, if you might help me focus the visions I'm having. Maybe they could give us a clue, and if I have another one I'd like to be able to focus on what's happening better."

"I'm not sure I can help or not, but it's worth a try. Is there anything specific that brings them on?" Zara relaxed a little now that she had something she could do.

"Oh, umm. I think maybe, uh..." Jules's cheeks went all hot. Her chest did too. She'd like to blame the heater in the house, but she knew full well it was because of her answer. Suck it up, peanut butter cup. "I think physical contact with Dax might help."

Dax didn't say a word. His eyebrows did the talking for

him. They were saying "Oh, really? Then come on over here."
He simply held out a hand for hers and didn't make it sexual
at all.

Too bad.

Ack.

What was wrong with her?

"Yes, this is good. It helps to have some sort of anchor to
your body." Zara's face flushed a little. "If you feel yourself
losing control, squeeze his hand. Better yet, Dax, I'd like you
to rhythmically squeeze Jules's hand. That will give her something to connect her to the here and now. Trust me."

"No problem." Dax gently and slowly opened and closed
his hand around Jules. "How's that?"

Squeak. Simply thinking about touching him had already
sent her mind into dirty-town. The way he paused at the
tightest part of the grip on her, released her hand quickly,
then squeezed it again had all her girly parts on overdrive. She
couldn't help but equate this movement to the way he would--

"Jules, are you all right? Is there a vision coming on? Your
eyes are all glazed over and you're breathing hard." Zara
tipped her head to the side and studied Jules's every reaction.
It was like being watched in a very intimate moment.

"I'm fine." The high pitch to her voice betrayed that lie.
"What's next?"

Zara grinned at her, all too knowingly. "Let the vision flow
through you."

"Hmm. I don't exactly know how to do that. It's not like I
can control them. I think someone else, whoever is behind all
of this, is pushing them at me."

"Lass, that doesn't make sense. Whoever has planned this
abduction wouldn't want you to see them."

"Right. Yeah. But I still think someone else is putting these things in my head." Jules barely finished the last syllable of her sentence before a hurricane slammed into her body and she was sucked into another world in her mind. Wind was blowing through her hair and she couldn't breathe. Her heart beat so hard she could feel it in her limbs. Especially her arms. Her right arm and hand especially.

Actually that pulse, pulse, pulse worked for her. It gave her something to focus on instead of the gale force winds blowing up her nose and down her throat. With each beat, the wind died down a notch and she could make out some shapes. Trees. Big pine trees and little shrubs and brush were blowing past her.

That wasn't right. She was moving past the trees, and the ground. This must be the reserve. She wasn't sure because the scenery went by so fast, but it was the closest woody area and she had the sense they weren't far from home.

Was she flying? No. Running. Only she wasn't the one running. Jules stared down and saw furry legs and paws beneath her. A wolf. Oh, and another one. And one more creature whose claws bore long sharp talons drifted over the ground along with the wolves.

A dragon. It wasn't running along with them, it was flying, but low enough to the ground it was almost level with the wolves. Jules couldn't seem to turn her head to see the dragon's body or face and the night hid the color of the scales so close to the ground. Was it red? Was this dragon Dax?

With each step the wolves ' paws took, they grew, and grew, and grew. Then there were no more steps to take and the wolves skidded to a stop in the stones and pebbles at the water 's edge. The dragon kept flying out over the water, skimming its talons along the crests of waves. She understood that some dragons actually liked the water and waited to see if this one dove in. Instead it circled back around and roared at her and the wolves. It blew a long stream of red hot fire over their heads, just like Dax had in her last vision.

Thank God for the beating of her heart grounding her or she'd be scared to death right now. That wasn't entirely right. It was more than just her heart. Something or someone else was keeping her from floating away, helping her stay in the vision.

A voice popped into her head. It was neither male nor female, high or low, soft or loud. *I need them.*

"Who are you? Why do you need them and what are you doing with the children?" Of course she didn't get an answer. The being, maybe it was a dragon, maybe it wasn't, didn't feel malevolent. It must be, though. Who stole children out of their homes when they were sleeping? It was ridiculous to think that this being didn't mean them any harm. "You need to let them go and leave us all alone."

The being turned its red eyes, glowing on Jules and the fire there burned so hot it was white. *You are not yet lost, yet you are not found. I'll see you again soon and then you will be gone.*

A wave of heat poured over Jules and the last thing she heard were the yips and yowls of the wolves at the beach. Her eyes burned and she didn't want to open them. Her heart raced, faster than the beating she'd thought was her heart. She grounded herself back in her body, consciously this time and soon she recognized the rhythmic squeezing of her hand.

Dax. He'd been with her all along. Thank God. "I'm here."

She heard long exhales of breath, the sound of several people relieved and breathing again. She didn't know who else had seen her get that vision, and the only way to find out was to finally open her eyes. When she did, Dax's amber eyes, with the glowing red fire banked behind them, pulled her all the way into the here and now.

He searched her face, checking to make sure she was okay, never once stopping his rhythmic pulses of his hand around hers. Jules squeezed his hand and held it tight. "I'm okay. I know where they are."

Gal squatted down beside Dax and grabbed Jules's leg. The streaks of tears tracks belied her extreme worry. "Where? Are they okay?"

"They're at the beach. I think they are okay. Whatever has taken them isn't hurting them."

Gal spun and burst into her wolf form, letting her clothes fall to the ground. She took off out of the kitchen and they all heard her howl from outside as she bolted into the night toward the beach.

Heli and Zara exchanged looks. Zara nodded and addressed Jules and Dax. "We'll grab the truck and bring the in-case-of-shifting emergency bags. Can you two get there on your own?"

Dax stood and pulled Jules up with him. "I'll fly us there. We'll be there before the rest of you and can scout the area. Jules can call you if there's trouble that we can't handle."

She shouldn't like the idea of flying into battle quite so much. She looked to Heli and Zara. "Do you have some sort of weapon I can use? I felt a bit defenseless last time."

Heli thought for a second. "I've got my tranq gun in the car, but I'd like to keep that. Gal didn't want firearms in the house with the kids. I think there's a baseball bat in the hall closet though."

Better than nothing. She didn't know how to use a gun very well anyway. Only what she'd seen in movies. "That will do. We'll see you there."

The four of them moved out quickly and before the ladies were in their truck, Dax was already in his dragon form and they were lifting off into the sky. "That way. Go through the reserve, I think that's where we were running before. Maybe we can catch some clues along the way to what or where the creature that took them is hiding."

Smart, lass. Dax banked and Jules closed her eyes for just a moment reveling in the wind whipping through her hair.

She really should have tried flying, or skydiving, or even wind surfing before. Moving so fast, riding the wind felt so right. For now, soaring through the air with a baseball bat at the ready was good enough. Maybe when this was all over she would ask Dax to take her up into the clouds and sunshine.

We've got company. Dax dipped his head and she spotted three huge wolves sprinting into the edge of the reserve and another smaller one leading the pack.

That 's the Troikas and Gal. She could tell they were going all out, top speed, and she and Dax would overtake them in another second. His flying speed was at least twice the wolves ' ground speed and she didn't think he was going as fast as he could.

Jules would feel good about getting to the children first. Even though they all recognized it wasn't her fault they 'd been kidnapped, she wanted to be the one to return the little tykes to their worried parents. This was the only family she knew and every time she thought about letting them down nausea rolled through her stomach.

Them I recognize. It 's the demon horde racing them I 'm worried about. Look in the shadows at the edge of the trees. Dax demonstrated where he wanted her to look by shooting a stream of flame into the underbrush. His aim was so precise that the plant life didn't even singe, but the demon wyrm hiding there erupted into flame and turned into a pile of ash.

Crap. Either they raced ahead and found the kids, making sure they were safe from the being, or they stayed and defended the wolf pack from the rear. Jules was fully prepared to give up the victory of being able to return the kids safely. But what if the being was some sort of dragon bent on harming the kids or the wolves?

The pack had helped defend against the Black Dragon once before, but they had mostly fought the demons, not the dragon himself. The other dragons who 'd come to town had done that. The pack could full well get there and be killed. She and Dax had to help save them.

The wolves below didn 't slow but the one in back, she thought it was Niko, dropped back and howled. He stalked into the dark woods and they heard crazy squawks and growls then an explosion of ash like a mini volcano.

Oh good. He got them. They could speed ahead and fight the real battle.

Not even close. There were a good dozen more forming a circle around Niko. He lunged and bit at them, but they used their wings to jump out of his reach. Several shot small flames, more like fiery spittle, at the wolf, singing his fur. Dax swooped down and skimmed so close to the ground Jules could reach her hand out and pick the blades of grass if she wanted.

She did not. She wanted to kick some demon ass back to where they 'd come from. God, she hoped that Max, Kosta and Gal would be okay and could save the babies. Get in close to that group, I 'm going to ”

Dax spit a large ball of flame at them and they exploded.

Hey. No fair. I was going to knock their blocks off.

Sorry, lass. You can have that one. A chuckle rumbled through his belly above her head and the vibrations were like a giant purr. Or a giant vibrator.

Jules rolled her eyes at herself and then repositioned so she could hold the bat with both hands. Dax flew in close to a demon hot on Niko 's tail and at the last second pulled up so the bastard 's head was right in the sweet spot. She swung and connected so hard its head detached from its body and went flying, turning into oily streaks of demon remains in the air.

Niko yipped a thanks and went off to tear into another group, while Dax circled around. *Home run, my sweet.*

Those things don 't seem that hard to kill. We 'll eviscerate them in no time. Yay, us.

You 're right, they die easily. Their greatest strength is their sheer number. Dax flapped his wings hard, gaining a little altitude and pointed her in the direction of the beach. The path between them, the wolves, and the children was so thick with demons it looked like the night sky and earth had been inverted.

One, two, three, four, five, six, seven, eight, nine, ten, a hundred demons. They were all going to die.

BATTER UP

A hundred and fifty-two demon wyrms, one alpha wolf, one dragon, and one human. Didn't sound like a very good equation to Dax. What it equaled was a big ole shit storm. Either the wolves he was sent to help were fucked, or he and Jules were.

"Dax. Oh my God. We can't fight that many demons, can we? You don't happen to have some other super duper power you haven't shown me yet, do you?"

No, lass. Fire, flight, and fury are my only weapons. We are in a lot of trouble, as are your friends. I'm open to suggestions if you've got any bright ideas besides throwing your baseball bat at them.

"Yikes. I only see two choices. Either we stay and Alamo our asses or we grab Niko and get ahead of them. He's at your three o'clock."

He didn't know what Alamo-ing meant, but it didn't sound good. She was right, though. It was stay and fight, or retreat and live to fight another day, and or another hour. A huge battle was coming regardless.

While Jules had done a great job at keeping his flying right in their last battle against these bastards, there was no way he could actually put her into danger fighting them. Especially not against odds like this. He needed to get her to safety and come up with a plan to stem the tide of demons coming at the wolf pack.

All on his own. He'd always been a part of a team. He and Steele had fought a group off here before, but the wolves had ended up saving the day. Steele had almost lost his life. If he'd called Cage, or even Steele, when he knew something was wrong, he'd at least have some backup. Now he was one dragon against the end of the world. Because if anything happened to Jules....

Damn it. Why and how he was so invested in her was frustrating the shit out of the warrior part of him. He wasn't even in his Prime. He shouldn't be feeling this way about any woman. It wasn't like he even wanted to settle down if he could. The reminder that Red Dragon Warriors didn't get mates was tattooed on his freaking soul. And he certainly shouldn't be thinking about it at a time like this. Seriously, his heart, and if he was honest, his dick needed to get out of this conversation.

Head back in the game. Warrior mode on.

He could turn back toward the houses and drop Jules off. The horde was moving forward, toward the wolves and the beach. She could run back to the house. Which was already compromised and not safe in the least. Even if she made it there on her own without attracting the notice of the wyrms, he couldn't be sure she'd be safe.

So that was out. Dax circled over the top of the horde, looking for any breaks in the line, any weakness in their defenses, and keeping one eye on Niko. He was kicking ass and not bothering to take names, but the demons continued to attack. They were moving as one, creepily hive-mind like. Since Jett's Demon Dragon Wyr had come into their powers and freed themselves from the Black Witch's control, the remaining demon wyrms acted much more controlled and coordinated than before. Gone were the days where they could be tricked. These things were nothing more than mindless death drones.

Which made them easier to kill, but there were more of them. It also meant someone used them as a weapon from behind a coward's curtain. Either the Black Witch or the Black Dragon, rulers of hell, were somewhere nearby. The odds were stacked so far against the good guys tonight a chunk of dread sunk into the pit of his stomach like a lump of coal coated in broken glass.

Quit thinking. The only choice was to get Jules out of here and defend the pack until reinforcements could arrive.

Jules. We need to grab Niko and get the fuck out of here. We can't hold this horde off on our own and I won't let Niko sacrifice himself in this battle in the dragon war.

"Oh, Niko is not going to like that. Can you carry him in one claw and me in the other? Far, far, away from his teeth?"

She was completely right. Niko was going to be pissed. But this wasn't the first time that Dax had carried Niko. He hoped the wolf part of him remembered that and would know that Dax was there to help not harm. He shifted his wings and Jules so that he could grab the wolf off the ground and get back into the sky, out of reach of the demon wyrms as quickly as possible.

The horde was already closing in on the other wolves and

Niko wasn't going to be able to hold off the group surrounding the him, even as a massive wolf, much longer anyway. Pissed or not, he would still be alive and the rest of the wolf-shifter world wouldn't be out for dragons ' hides for causing their alpha's death.

He flew in on a silent draft, not wanting to give Niko any warning of this plan. At the very last second he grabbed the wolf around the shoulders and shot an arc of flame at the demons closing in. The wolf howled and growled and snapped its teeth.

Jules held up her hands, palms out and made soothing sounds, like she would a child, but they didn't help. Niko snapped his jaws at her and wriggled so that Dax was close to dropping him. *Hold still, wolf. We're saving your life and the lives of your family, so knock it off.*

The wolf growled, then shifted, finding his own grip on Dax's claw. "What's your plan, Red?"

Get to the kids, get them out of here. Regroup. Call for reinforcements.

"Not good enough. Your demons are a threat to my entire territory. My people, humans and beasts alike, are not prepared for a battle. They've barely recovered from the last one."

Like I told Jules, I'm open to suggestions. Lass? She might not be a warrior, but so far had kept a very cool head in the midst of overwhelming odds. He'd love to hear any ideas she might have on how the hell to get them out of this shitshow.

Niko harrumphed. "She is covering her eyes and appears to not be able to hear us."

"I can hear you fine. I'm trying to avoid looking at your nakedness."

Fucking wolves. The magic they used to shift was not the same as dragons. They burst out of their god-damned clothes every time they went between forms. Thank the First Dragon and the White Witch dragons were a bit more refined than that. Dax turned his claw to the side, even if it was an awkward position to face Niko away from her view.

Jules body shook with laughter. Wait. He didn't hear the sweet sound of her giggling. Fuck. She was convulsing, which meant another vision. He needed to land. Now.

He scanned the ground, looking for any safe place, or even a spot he could defend. There was nothing. The ground writhed with the bodies of a full-on demon wyrm stampede. They were moving fast now that none of them were distracted by fighting. The black beasts torpedoed toward the wolves and beach.

Fuck. He sure as shit could use a Gold Dragon around now to give them a boost from the wind. He had only his wings and his will to rely on. This was what he was trained for - saving the world. Even if that meant one human woman at a time. Dax rhythmically tapped one of his talons against Jules's leg hoping it would have the same effect as squeezing her hand did. He had no idea if he helped or not.

"Dude. She is glowing, like light is pouring out of her eyes. Red light." Niko's voice sounded both awed and worried. "Find my brothers and drop me. We'll meet you at the beach."

Dax pulled up a reserve of energy he didn't even know he had and put on a burst of speed. He found a sweet spot on a current and the horde fell behind. The other wolves came into view and Dax dropped quickly to get to them. He would get to the beach a lot faster if he wasn't carrying two passengers. Niko obviously felt the same. He shifted back into his wolf form a meter above the ground as Dax flew in low. He opened his claw and dropped the wolf at the front of the pack.

Niko hit the ground running, the power of his alpha showing. The other wolves couldn't keep up with him. Even with Niko's speed, Dax beat his wings hard, found that air current again and left the wolves behind. The beach came into view within seconds.

Hang on, Jules. We're almost there. A puff of wind pushed him from behind and Dax barreled toward the ground. He tucked Jules in close to his body, wrapped his wings around her and made a controlled crash onto his back onto the stony pebbled beach. He skidded to a stop, holding her tight.

"Well, that's one way to land, I guess."

Phew. Dax's heart began beating again. *Are you okay? What did you see?*

And can it help them not die in about five minutes from now?

"Yeah. I'm fine. Thanks for grounding me again. I felt you tapping my leg. It was a weird one, but I know that if we get the kids off the beach, they or it, or something will take care of the demon dragons."

Take care of? That sounded fishy. All of Jules's visions had been helpful so far, it would be stupid of him to doubt one of them now. He scanned the beach and didn't see anyone, pups or toddlers. Maybe those two young punks over there had scared them away. If they'd harmed the little ankle-biters, Dax would destroy them. He rolled and carefully and opened his claw so Jules could climb out.

The second she was on her feet she made a mad dash toward the punks. "Tristan, Ellie."

Uh. Seriously? The two kids standing on the beach were barely prepubescents. If they were the Troika 's pups, there was some insanely powerful magic going on here. Like beyond what any of them knew the Black Witch could do. She had no control over life. She was the Queen of the Dead. Who else would the Black Dragon be working with that had this kind of power? He couldn't imagine who or what would want baby brains in the bodies of pre-teens.

Dax shifted and ran after Jules, eyeing the kids and looking for signs they were who Jules thought they were. He also looked for signs of dark magic, like shadows that were too long, too dark, or not where they were supposed to be. The moon was high and full, so there were plenty of shadows, but none out of place. They were perfect places for the demons to pop out of as soon as they figured out where the kids were.

"Jules? Did you shrink?" The girl addressed Jules and obviously knew who she was. She was wearing an oversized leather vest and leggings big enough she had to hold them up with her hand. They looked well worn, but not by this young lady. They barely fit her.

The young man had on nothing but a pair of shorts decorated with those colorful, round Christmas ornament bulbs all over them. Kids were weird. Or these weren't kids at all. Dax narrowed his eyes at the boy, who glared right back at him.

"Jules. Be careful." She was too trusting that these were the Troikas and that they wouldn't hurt her. If they were tainted by the forces of hell.

"No, honey, you've gotten bigger. A lot bigger." Jules slowed and approached the pair a bit more cautiously now.

Tristan picked up a piece of driftwood and held it aloft like a sword. "Ellie, stand back. We don't know who these people are. They could be the ones she warned us about. She said they would take on a disguise to look like people we know, to garner our trust."

Garner their trust? Who talked like that? Especially a child.

"Tristan." Jules stood very still and bowed her head slightly, smartly showing this young man her throat, which was a sign of submission to wolves. He turned his eyes to watch her approach, studied her, but didn't move to attack.

He couldn't hurt the kids, but he wasn't going to let them hurt Jules either. He approached the young man. He wouldn't show his throat to him. Whether this was the Troika boy or not, he needed to understand that there were bigger and badder monsters in the world and that he needed to decide who was an ally and who wasn't.

"Son, We are here to help you. But you need to make a decision. There's a horde of demon wyrms coming this way and there is very little way we can defend you and ourselves from them in this position. The water doesn't help us and while I can keep them held back for a while with my flame, ultimately we will go down. We must retreat. Look into your heart, you know this woman. She cares for you. She will never let any harm come to you or your sister."

Tristan glanced warily between the people around them. The blue spark of his wolf soul shined through his eyes as he considered what Dax said. By the way he was still holding that stick like a sword, he didn't look apt to believe anyone. Just like an alpha wolf. That more than anything helped Dax to believe this was the son of Maxsim Troika, alpha of the Grimm pack.

The girl touched him on the arm. She was no shy flower this one. That alpha glow was in her eyes too. "We should trust them. Something bad is coming. She said so."

"Who is this she you keep referring too?" Jules used each interaction with them to move closer.

The girl stared at Jules for a minute trying to decide if she should trust her with the answer or not. "The woman in red."

Who the fuck is the woman in red. Wasn't that a song? It certainly wasn't an answer. "Can you give us anything more than that? Is she someone we and your family need to be worried about?"

The kids exchanged looks and used some sort of communication that only the two of them understood. It could be mindspeak like shifters used, but as far as he knew, none could use it in their human forms. Maybe it was one of those twin connection things. Dax used the opportunity to check the perimeter and move closer to Jules. The time to placate these kids was going to run out soon. He needed to figure out how he was going to get the three of them out of here if the wolves didn't show up before the demons. "Tell us on the move, kids. We need to get you out of here and to safety."

The girl shook her head. "She said not to move from the beach until we got the signal. It's not safe."

No shit, Sherlock. "That sounds like a trap. Demon wyrms are stampeding their way here right now. If we don't get you off the beach, we're all dead."

"Then go."

"Not on your life, kid. Literally. It is my duty to protect you and her, and everyone else from the demon plague. I will fight to the death if needs be."

That made the boy's eyes go wide. "You don't owe us your life. Why would you do that?"

"Because warriors protect the world from evil."

Just then evil showed up.

Demon wyrms rose up in the shadows, forming a wall in

front of them. "Get behind me and stay near the water. These beasts are made in the pits of hell and don't like the water."

Dax shifted into his dragon form and blew a long, bright flame at the growing front row of demons.

Watch, dragon. Don't singe the fur. Niko's voice popped into his head. The wolves bounded into the fray and tore demon dragons limb from limb. One smaller grey wolf burst through the line and straight for Jules and the kids behind Dax. She didn't shift, but jumped up on the girl and then the boy and licked their faces.

"Mom. Gross. Stop it. We're a little busy here if you didn't notice." She yipped and pushed the kids behind her, turned and growled at the oncoming line wyrms. A few of them actually slowed their attack recognizing their own deaths in her eyes.

Never piss off a mama wolf.

The children shifted into their wolves too and while their mother didn't let them get past her, they did snap and growl at any demons that even looked their way.

Jules was the only vulnerable human left. *Lass, climb up on my back. I can keep you safer out of reach of the demons and the shadows.*

"Okay, but I'm not riding you."

We'll save that for later.

Jules smacked his side and then clambered up with a lift up from Dax's wing. "I'm getting a crossbow or something if this is going to be a regular occurrence. On your six - two wyrms coming in."

Dax smacked the demons away with his tail and sent them careening into the ocean. They sizzled and sank into the waves.

"Oh my God. Dax, who or what is that? It doesn't look like

the others." Jules pointed her baseball bat toward a clump of demons to the right.

No. That wasn't a clump. It was one bigger demon. A mutant demon wyrm? A Demon Dragon who did not escape the spell of the Black Witch?

It threw its head back and roared and that's when Dax saw the collar. Fuck. It wasn't a demon at all. It was a Gold dragon.

WE'RE GONNA NEED A BIGGER BOAT

*O*oh. Dax was about to blow his top. Which was both sexy and scary. She wasn't sure if he was mad that a Gold Dragon was fighting with the demons or that the Gold was being forced to fight on the side of the demons. He'd explained really quickly that a bunch of Golds had been captured and were under the control of an evil succubus queen.

That sounded really horrible. Jules knew about such a small little bit of the supernatural world. She had to think a minute about what a succubus even did. Next someone would tell her unicorns were real, too.

If they were, she was so going to make Dax introduce her to one.

Dax bounded into the fray, spraying fiery death all over the baddies. This riding on top of him thing was not exactly comfortable. His scales were chafing the inner thighs of her jeans and it wasn't like she had anything to hold onto other than a ring and a prayer.

That and her baseball bat. Dax growled and tore into a

group of demons moving in on Gal and the pups. He side-swiped the lot of them with his huge tail and flipped one up in the air. Perfect. She used its head for batting practice. So far she was batting a thousand.

There was something wrong with her for enjoying seeing the little wyrms explode into ash and oil. A warm fuzzy feeling she never would have associated with a battle against demons in a supernatural war warmed her insides the same way Dax's kiss had earlier. Which she totally needed to stop thinking about. It didn't mean anything. He was a warrior. She was a chubby babysitter.

Not exactly a match made in heaven.

He was here to do a job, which included finding out who was sending her visions. That was the only reason he was sticking so close to her. It wasn't because he was attracted to her. Yeah. She needed to keep telling herself that so when he dropped her like it's hot tomorrow or the next day, like good-looking dudes always did, it wouldn't hurt so much.

It was just a crush. Brought on by the adrenaline of fighting monsters. She'd get over it. Just like she had every other crush she'd ever had. Because love and relationships were not for her. They were for pretty and interesting women. Like the mates of the Troikas.

She was fine with that. There were lots of other things she could do with her life. Like maybe learning to be a demon spotter for dragon warriors. She was pretty damn good at that. "Two on your four, three coming in on your two."

That sentence shouldn't even make sense, but Dax reacted as if the two of them were some super elite Navy SEALs or Army Rangers or something. She and Dax worked as a team. They were connected. There went those warm fuzzies in her chest again.

Ignore it. She lifted the bat up over her head and swung it in a circle, hollering, "Wahoo. You demons are going down. Bring 'em on, Dax."

The wall of demons was getting thicker by the moment and she'd lost sight of the Gold dragon. Dax had to protect the wolf pups and Galyna, but she knew he wanted to get to that dragon they were using as a gladiator. Jules wasn't helping kill demons much, she could at least keep an eye out for Dax's friend in this fray.

She got to her knees and scanned the area. Four wolves were fighting their way toward the beach from the east, leaving a mangled mass of demon remains in their wake. They'd make it to the beach soon. She still couldn't see enough. Dax bounded forward to repel a bold group and Jules almost fell off.

Her shoelaces got caught on one of Dax's scales, saving her from tumbling down his back. She lost hold of her bat, though.

Babe, you all right?

He did not need his attention divided. "Fine. Don't worry about me."

She tugged her lace from under the scale and that gave her the perfect idea. She crossed her fingers this wouldn't hurt him. Jules yanked her shoes off and shoved her toes under one of his scales, then did the same with another one so her feet were shoulder width apart. His skin was hot under her feet, but she could use her toes to grip and hopefully keep her balance.

Very carefully she moved into a crouch. When Dax jerked to the side to avoid some fire spittle from the demons, she moved with him. Cool. She pushed up, stayed half bent over until she found her balance and then stood all the way up. Yes.

From this vantage point she could see the whole beach and the entire horde. Gulp. There were so many of them. They weren't even making a dent in their numbers. For every demon Dax and the wolves killed, more popped up out of the shadows. This was bad. Really, really bad.

They were gonna need a bigger boat.

Or an escape plan. Her vision had said if they got the kids out of there, the demon wyrms would go. But did that mean because they were going to be following the kids? She didn't have enough information. She also didn't see another choice.

"Dax, we have to get the kids out of here."

We can't leave the wolf pack to fend for themselves. You and Galyna go. We'll cover you.

No way. She searched the area again for anything or anyone that could help them. "We need a distraction. Then we can all get away."

There. The Gold Dragon was a hundred yards away and moving toward the beach. It too had a woman hiding herself behind a black cloak and hood on its back who was holding onto some sort of collar around its neck and harness holding its wings down. She pointed at Jules and the dragon blew a huge gust of wind, knocking all the demon dragons in their path down.

Jules crouched and prepared herself to get hit by the blast, but it died into nothing more than a strong breeze whipping her hair across her face. The woman yelled something and smacked the dragon on its head. It turned and growled at her.

"I don't think she has full control of him. He pulled that punch. We can free him and get our distraction in the process."

I agree she doesn't have control. She's caged his wings and I bet if we can sever those bonds, he can fly and be free of her.

"Right. You two take to the air. That's the distraction. I got it. Be right back." She slid down off Dax's back and over to Gal. "Can you communicate with Max and the other wolves? We need to free that Gold Dragon. Can they go claw or bite the leather straps holding his wings down?"

Gal nodded and was silent for a moment. Then she yipped which clearly meant yes.

"Okay, good. When he's free and takes to the air, Dax will do the same, which will cause a huge ole distraction. We all need to run then. Retreat to..."

Too late to finish the plan. The wolves used the opening in the line of demons and ran toward the Gold Dragon as if he were the enemy. God, she hoped they understood he was one of the good guys. They jumped at him, two going for his back and wings. The smaller wolf who was Selena attacked the woman on the dragon 's back.

Whoa. She was going straight for the jugular for real. The woman and wolf went down to the ground and the Gold Dragon lurched back. He shook to get the wolves off his back and Max went flying. Dax bellowed, getting the other dragon's attention and must have said something to him because he settled down and held still. In moments, Niko and Kosta had the bindings broken and the Gold dragon spread huge wings, roaring so loud it sounded like a bomb exploded.

That was the signal to retreat if she'd ever heard one. Jules cupped her hands and shouted to Gal and the pups. "Go, run, run, run."

Dax and the Gold both lifted up into the air and the wolves bolted down the beach away from the battle.

Please, please, please let the kids and Max be okay. Jules watched and waited for them to appear. The children were soon flanked by Niko and Kosta, who had very little trouble protecting their sides from stray demons. One or two flew at them in their weird hopping bat-like way and were eviscerated almost instantly.

Still no Max or anyone else, but the plan was working. The two dragons above her head were working together, Dax shooting fire and the Gold one spreading it across the masses with gusts of wind. Demons were exploding into ash in droves.

And still more came. Where were they all coming from? Out of the shadows, of course, there were unending droves of them. Those two dragons were not going to be enough to stem the tide. Two demons stalked toward her. Crud. She'd sent all of her defenses running or flying away. She backed up toward the water. Dax had said these things didn't like it. The waves washed over her feet and still they came at her.

The baseball bat she'd dropped earlier brushed against her leg, bobbing in the water. She reached for it and one of the demons attacked. There was no way she'd swing the bat in time to avoid getting her face bitten off. She was going to die. She screamed, crying out for the one thing she was going to miss most when she was dead. "Dax!"

He swooped down and the world went into slow motion. The demon wyrm reached out its claws and opened its jaw wide. She could see each and every one of its big black teeth dripping with disgusting demon slobber. Behind it, the big Red Dragon with fire in his eyes tucked his wings flying at her so fast, and yet so slow.

Jules turned her head and she saw everything. Like everything. But through a lens, like she wasn't really there. The succubus had the woman in red pinned to the ground with wisps of red magic. Max was struggling to get out of a pile of demons biting and tearing at his fur. The Gold Dragon's mind was dark and shattered, only barely holding onto reality. The Troika twins were pups and babies, and fierce warriors all at the same time. The demons were nothing more than empty husks with dark magic inside of them.

A huge black dragon, or was it red, who was very, very old lay beneath their feet with that same emptiness in the place where his soul should be. A goddess, who loved death, held him with strings like a puppet and he screamed, trying to scratch at them.

Dax's chest burned with a fire brighter than the sun. It was the most beautiful thing she'd ever seen and she wanted nothing more than to touch it, wrap herself up inside of the fire and live there with him. A light inside of her own soul reached out for his fire, but he couldn't see her.

Either she was already dead or she needed to face up to the fact that she had a drug problem. She didn't even like mushrooms.

"I did say we should have given her the necklace last night. Now she's all confused and doesn't even have her dragon to help her make sense of it all." A melodic voice she sort of recognized sounded from someplace behind her.

She didn't see anyone else. There was a blinding white light blocking her vision though. The only thing she could see now was a dragon, easily twice the size of either Dax or the Gold. This one had scales that were every color of the rainbow.

Fine, fine, my love. You were right. The dragon licked a woman's face. Wait. Maybe he was kissing her? The voice was definitely coming from him. It didn't seem intended for her mind like Dax's did. *Give it to her now and I'll take care of these Galla demons for them. They could use a break.*

The woman turned to Jules and tilted her head to the side.

"She's much more powerful than we thought. That's what we get for not finding a father to protect her all these years."

Oh no. The succubus was a powerful one. Jules sent up a silent prayer that everyone wasn't irrevocably harmed by her. The wolf pack had fought so long and hard to make Rogue a safe place. It would seriously suck if they lost their mother now. It would make Jules incredibly sad too. They had welcomed her into the pack when she was feeling low and alone. She didn't know her own parents and had always thought of the pack matriarch as a sort of surrogate mother.

The dragon lifted up into the air and shot flame after flame at the masses of demons surrounding them. He made a weird sound that might have been a giggle.

The woman stepped in front of Jules and looked her up and down, then patted her on the shoulder. "Don't worry, dear. Those Gallas aren't going to hurt anyone else. Kur will take care of them. Now, let's talk about you."

"Me?" Whoa. She could move and talk again. The dream-like state still surrounded them, but Jules could now operate independently, unlike her other visions. She had a hard time focusing on anything other than the woman. She had beautiful tawny skin and huge almond-shaped eyes, similar to Gal's gorgeous Middle Eastern looks. Her long hair flowed around them in waves as if it had a mind of its own. The goddess of love couldn't be any more beautiful. There was also a fierceness about her, too. She was no gentle grandmother.

"Yes. You and your destiny."

"I have a destiny? I'm just a plain old human. We don't have destinies." She'd never really believed in fate. She didn't want to because it was too scary to think hers might be to never have a family of her own. Even if that was what she believed somewhere in the deepest recesses of her heart. That place she didn't share with anyone.

"Of course you do. Humans have all kinds of fabulous fates. I should know. But you're not a plain old human. Not if you don't want to be."

"What do you mean?"

"You're something very special. I've suppressed your powers for a long time. They seem to have started to leak through. Someone has awakened them." She waggled her eyebrows like that was supposed to mean something to Jules.

Powers. She had powers. "You mean the visions? I thought someone else was sending those to me."

The woman's face was clearly an expression of duh. "Yes and no. Someone very naughty is sending those your way. You're a witch, with a touch of second sight. I gave that ability out a little too freely at the beginning. I've learned my lesson since then."

Yeah, right. "No way. I tried a little witchcraft. I couldn't even make fake spells from the magic emporium work. I can't do a magic trick to save my life."

The woman smiled, not in a patronizing way, but with understanding and empathy. She touched a lock of Jules's hair and stroked it like a mother would. The adoration in her eyes had Jules almost falling over with how beautiful the woman made her feel. "You're not that kind of witch. Humans are funny with their notions of black cats and pointed hats. Your magic is that of the elements, passed down from gods and goddesses of my time."

"Like earth, wind, and fire?" She thought of the fire in Dax's eyes and hoped that was her element.

"No, that's a band. Your friend Fleur is an earth witch, the mermaid you'll meet soon is a water witch, when the four elements are combined you get something new, a white witch whose true power is love and emotions. Ciara is still working on that. She'll get it eventually. She has to." The woman, or witch, or goddess looked a bit pensive when she mentioned the last woman.

"Are there red witches?"

"Mmm." She stared into the distance for a minute, but at nothing that Jules could see. She sighed and then snapped back into a smile and looked at Jules again. "You're a Gold witch, which means you can use the power of the sun and the wind. Try it."

Sun and wind. So not fire. She sounded like a witch who liked to hang out at the beach. Which was exactly what she was doing right now. She did love a good warm summer day with a breeze blowing through her hair. "How?"

"I'm a fan of the swish and flick." The woman held out her hand and swirled her hand about in a sort of figure eight.

"Don't I need a magic spell or a word?" Like wingardium leviosa or something.

"The sun and wind are already a part of you and you don't need to do anything but look inside yourself and find them. Then use the elements like you'd use your arms or legs or brain."

Jules closed her eyes and didn't see anything different than she normally did. Just the inside of her eyelids. She sighed and thought about how to tell the woman there was nothing there. She was mistaken and Jules wasn't anything special. She knew it.

The Goddess whispered in her ear. "Look deeper."

"I am. There's nothing...." A tiny flicker, like a candle being lit very far away, formed in her mind's eye. She stared as it got bigger and bigger. The flicker wasn't random either. It pulsed, like the beat of a heart. Like the rhythm Dax had tapped against her leg and used when he'd squeezed her hand. Jules wanted to hold the light, wrap it up in a hug, and tell it that she loved it.

"There it is. Easy peasy." She lifted Jules's arm so it was held straight out from her body. "Open your eyes."

Jules opened her eyes and found a huge ball of light in the palm of her hand and the wind whipping through her hair. An incredible rush warmed her from the inside out as if the sun were shining inside of her.

"You've found your true self in there. Good job. Now pull on that and give the power a shove at that Galla demon." She pointed to a group of gross mouth-breather demons in front of her.

Jules swished her fingers and the light burst from her fingers and smacked the demon in the chest. There was no explosion, not even a pile of oil and ash. It simply disappeared. "Where did it go?"

The goddess made a hilarious ugly face. "They are born of black magic, hatred, and shadows. The best way to destroy them is the light."

The colorful dragon did a loopty-loop over them. "Then why is your dragon shooting fireballs at them?"

"He likes to." She shrugged and grinned with a whole lot of love in her eyes. "Yours does too. The hatred for the Black Dragon isn't seated as deeply in his heart as his brothers. That's because of you and your light, you know?

Jules snapped her head back and forth between the goddess and the slow-mo movements of Dax half frozen in the air. "Me? What do I have to do with it?"

You didn't tell her yet? Come on. I'm gonna call him spoiler alert. The rainbow dragon came in for a landing next to the Goddess.

She patted his snout. "Silly dragon."

Maybe it will finally get a fire lit under the redling 's ass. He needs his mate.

"And she needs him." The goddess got that same far away wistful sad look from before.

So then get on with it already. Give her the necklace and let's be on our way. Jara is a little too close for comfort on this one and he's gonna throw a fit after all his Galla Demons go missing. He always was a drama llama.

"I know. It won't take long for him to find out. That succubus is here. Stupid girl."

Where? I'll eat her up and spit out her bones.

"That's sweet, my love. Maybe next time." She turned back to Jules and a placed her hands on her shoulders. "Jules Heulwen, I restore and unveil your true powers and dub thee a dragon daughter. Make us proud."

The goddess slipped a shining gold necklace over Jules's head with a pendant shaped like the sun that rested right over her heart. A flash of gold and red light sparkled and the world snapped back to life.

Jules, lass. I thought I lost you. Dax swooped down and surrounded Jules with his wings. In a breath he shifted back into his human form and was holding her in his arms. A bright light shined from his chest underneath his shirt.

Jules blinked and swallowed. She had no idea what had just happened to her, but she felt different on the inside. Warmer. Stronger. Like she could do anything. The wind whipped through her hair and even in the dark of night rays of sunshine poured down from the sky like spotlights. The demon wyrms nearest them disappeared into nothingness.

Dax looked around and together they watched the entire horde disintegrate in the light of Jules's sunshine. The entire army of demons was there, and then gone as the light spread across the land. In its wake the only life was Selena, standing over the prone body of Max on one side of them, and the hulking body of a severely injured Gold Dragon on the other.

Gal and the wolf pups must have been hiding nearby because they and the other alpha wolves rushed toward Max and Selena. A pickup truck skidded onto the beach not a moment later. Heli and Zara jumped out, one with a bag of blankets and clothes, and the other with a huge shotgun cocked and ready to rock.

Jules wanted to go to them, but she needed a minute to breathe and figure out what had just happened. She wavered on her feet and the light around them faded. Dax caught her before she could fall and held her tight. She laid her head on his chest, but something hot poked against her face.

Dax looked down at his chest, then into Jules's eyes. He pulled out the crystal pendant hanging around his neck and the glow surrounded them in heat and light. The golden necklace matched with its own powerful beams like sunshine. The light mingled and danced together all around them. "How can this be? You're the one. My mate."

From somewhere behind the Gold Dragon they heard a woman's scream. "Noooo."

MINE

*M*ark.
Claim.
Mate.

Something very strange had happened on this beach. He didn't just mean how Jules had called on the sun and eviscerated an entire horde of demon wyrms, saving them all. That was some serious crazy power. She'd pulled so much light down from the sky and thrown it around like confetti. Killer confetti.

The battle had lasted all night and now the early light of morning was touching the world.

While he'd been fighting off the horde, wondering how in the hell they were going to escape with their lives with the odds stacked against them so severely, Jules had gone from hot chick, to literally hot. She had been glowing.

At first he'd thought it had been another vision, but then he'd started hearing voices too. She was talking to another woman. One that Dax couldn't see through the white light surrounding her. What he did see was the biggest, most powerful dragon, with scales every color of the rainbow doing aerial acrobatics and destroying chunks of the demons like it was fun.

In between each shot, he looked straight at Dax and laughed. At least Dax thought that's what the dragon had done. But why would it do that? It wasn't laughing at him, more like talking but without words.

Words had stuck in his head though and he had no doubt as to their meaning.

Mark. Claim. Mate.

Make Jules his.

How could he? Match, the Red Dragon Wyvern, didn't have his mate yet and until he did, the rest of the reds were shit out of luck. Weren't they?

Dax held Jules tight in his arms. She was his mate. He knew it. He didn't understand how it could possibly be, but he knew all the way down to the very core of his soul she was his and he was hers.

That scared the holy bejeezus out of him. Dax held Jules tight in his arms, never wanting to let her go. She melted into him, but then jerked her head away and stared at the light coming from underneath his shirt.

He looked down at his chest, then into her eyes. The soul shard hanging around his neck that contained a sliver of his soul mixed with that of the First Dragon glowed, surrounding them in heat and light. It was every dragon's most precious possession. It gave them the ability to shift between dragon and man and was a gift directly from the White Witch. It was part of how every dragon knew who and what he was, why he was here. It was a physical manifestation of his own inherent value in the world. It was also how a dragon knew he was in the presence of his true mate. The true love the

First Dragon and the White Witch shared was contained in every dragon's soul and it recognized the one being in the world who was perfect to be a compliment and boon to their own soul.

He'd ignored its glow before. Deep down he'd never believed he would ever find true love. Red dragons carried a black mark on their souls that the rest of the dragon wyrs knew nothing about. The only others that could ever understand were the Demon Dragons. Which was probably why most Red Dragons avoided them. They saw too much of their own shadow selves in the faces of their half-brothers from hell.

It drove the Reds to defend the world against the darkness. Because they understood what it was, what it meant. With that mark marring them, the Red Dragons would be the ones to truly recognize the darkness of the Black Dragon.

A Red Dragon was destined to defeat the Black Dragon. They all knew it, but not one of them knew which dragon would have to sacrifice himself for the cause.

The golden necklace around Jules's throat matched the light coming from Dax's soul shard with its own powerful beams like sunshine. The light mingled and danced together all around them. His beautiful, smart, fierce mate. "How can this be? You're the one. My mate."

"Noooo." A woman's voice that Dax would recognize anywhere forever more screamed. "You are mine."

He shoved Jules behind him and prepared to defend her against the vile evil who wanted a piece of him. "You have no claim on me, Geshtianna."

The Succubus Queen stepped out from behind the Gold Dragon who lay on the ground injured, but not unconscious. She wore a long red dress more fitting a royal ball than a battlefield. Aha. The mysterious woman in red. Mystery solved

The Gold Dragon's eye followed her, but it did not move. She still had it under her control. "No? We'll see about that, my red lover."

Jules peeked her head out from behind him and that's when Geshtianna made her move. The force of her lust poured out of her in waves that made the Gold Dragon roar and sent Dax to his knees. The light from his shard dimmed and pulled back into the pendant.

"You cannot trick me with your false emotions, succubus. This shard, my soul, my heart already belongs to another." He knew it. But did Jules? She was attracted to him. He recognized the scent of sexual attraction at least. He hadn't been the best protector for her and he'd beg her forgiveness for that every day if he could. If the two of them survived this battle, he would mark her, claim her, and beg her to be his mate.

"I don't see your mark on anyone. If you had a mate, I would not be able to have this effect on you. Why don't you come over here and mark me, give me that soul shard? You know you want to."

Dax gritted his teeth and held every muscle in his body still, resisting her pull. He couldn't help his body's response, including the tightening in his pants, but he would not give in to her. Not when he'd only just found Jules. There was no way he would ever be with any woman other than his mate ever again. "No."

A golden glow surrounded Dax and Jules stepped out from behind him and blocked Geshtianna's advance. "Back off, cray-cray lady. This dragon warrior is mine."

He was. Fuck, yeah. The light at his chest renewed, the spark inside fighting to get out and to his mate. With a gargantuan effort, Dax lifted one knee and set his foot on the ground.

Jules turned, grabbed Dax's face between her hands and laid the most sensuous, hot kiss of his entire life on him. Their tongues danced and she tasted of ripe peaches and sweet buttery cream. His cock had been thickening before, now it was bursting to get out of his pants and into her. He'd never wanted anyone so much in his life.

Jules broke the kiss with his lower lip between her teeth. She nipped at him, sighed and opened her eyes. "Sorry. I hope that wasn't too forward. I like you. I'd like to see where this goes. So tell me now if you belong to another and I'll back off."

"I'm yours, if you'll have me." Please let her be his.

"Don't go all stalker obsessive on me." She winked and then gave him another quick kiss. Then she pointed her arm at Geshtianna and formed a ball of light in her hand. The wind whipped around all of them and she rose up into the air like she was Captain Marvel. "He is mine."

Geshtianna scoffed. "Not if he hasn't claimed you. He's free game and I want him. These golds are missing that certain something I'm looking for in a lover. They lack the darkness of a red dragon whose blood is so much more delicious for it."

The golden sunlight bathed Jules's entire body and poured forth from her eyes. "Far be it for me to judge anyone's kinks, lady. But you got issues and should maybe see a therapist about that. He is not yours. He may not have yet claimed me, but I claim him. So back the fuck off."

"I am not afraid of your little light display and I am not a lady. I am the Succubus Queen and you will submit to me." Another wave of lust power smacked into them and the Gold Dragon lumbered to its feet.

Uh-oh. The Gold's eyes were hazy and he growled deep

and low. That guy was one angry dragon. Under Geshtianna's control it could easily snap any human, or dragon in human form, in two with one snap of his jaw. He turned his big head toward Jules and rose up on his hind legs. It looked like he would attack, but instead exposed his soft underbelly to her. A dark hole swirled in the middle of his chest, right over his heart.

Jules gasped, glared at Geshtianna and threw all the light she was carrying directly at the Gold Dragon. He absorbed everything she had and stretched out his wings. The collar around his neck burned away and fell to the ground.

Anger, stoked by fear tainted Geshtianna's allure."Damn it. You will all submit to me."

Behind them in the water, the very first rays of the sun streaked across the sky. The Succubus Queen gurgled and threw her arm up to shield her eyes from the rays swimming around them and joining Jules's pure light. If ever there was a time to take Geshtianna out, it was now.

He couldn't hurt her the same way he had before. His regular Red Dragon powers weren't powerful enough on their own. Dax opened that dark part of him he usually kept hidden from the world and let the power there flow through him. His dragon form burst forth and the fire inside of him boiled from his mouth.

Dax lunged at the succubus and pinned her to the ground. He opened his claw and let his sharp talons slice through the hair at Geshtianna's neck, stopping right at her jugular. She pushed at him with her allure. It didn't even tickle him. The black mark on his soul couldn't be influenced by the likes of her. If she knew its darkness she would be the one who was afraid.

The blackness rolled through him and burned hot,

pouring his threat out like burnt sludge. He barely recognized his own dragon voice. *Now you will submit to me, you bloodsucking leech. We've foiled your plot to steal the wolf pups and my amazing mate has freed your slave. Now you die by my hand.*

Geshtianna hissed, fear stark in her eyes. She raked at his claws with her hands, trying to loosen his hold on her throat. Desperation came out in her blather. "Not if you ever want to know where the rest of the gold dragon slaves are. Every gold dragon and every succubus who holds their chain are under my thrall. Kill me now and they die, starving and lost in the blackness of the underworld. A horrible way to die, don't you think?"

Fucking hell. He had her by the throat, but she had him by the balls. He couldn't let the Golds live out their days in horror. He'd seen already what that meant and he would do almost anything to free them.

Where are they? He pressed the tip of one talon into the flesh at her neck. There would be no backing down this day.

The utter fear melted out of her eyes and she replaced her mask of sensual control. She knew the move was hers to make. "I'll never tell the likes of you. You're shit out of luck, little Red."

No, but I know all your secrets, Queen. The Gold Dragon, fully restored to his full powers, set down beside Dax, no longer a prisoner of war. There was a new peace to his eyes. Whatever spell the Succubus Queen had over him was gone. *I will lead the dragon warriors to Geshtianna's lair and free our brethren. There lies the secret to defeating the Black Witch and her plans to use the new generation for her own gain.*

His voice and countenance were so calm and collected, that Dax was completely taken by surprise when the dragon pushed him out of the way, freeing Geshtianna from his grip. *You will never have control over any man or beast ever again.*

The Queen screamed and threw every ounce of her power out, fighting tooth, nail, and allure for her life. The Gold lifted the succubus into the air with one claw and very simply reached out and sliced Geshtianna's head off her body in one quick motion.

He breathed a sigh of relief and a shimmer of light that signaled his shift from dragon to man washed over him.

Holy shit. Dax stared down at Zon, the master at arms of the Gold Dragon Wyr. "You and your mate have saved me, Red. I thank you."

Dax tugged at the darkness he'd called on to retreat back down now that the threat was eliminated. It took a minute, but with one look at his beautiful Jules and the black hole retreated all on its own. He was once again able to shift into his human form. He pulled her into a quick kiss that held a promise for later. When she was breathless, he released her and then clasped the freed dragon's arms.

Zon responded by pulling Dax into a huge dragon hug and whispered to him. "Mark and claim your mate now, before any more danger can befall either of you. Give her your soul so that both of you may be safe from the machinations of the underworld."

Good idea. Dax noticed that Zon's own soul shard was missing. Had it been taken in Hell by the succubus Portia or had he found his mate in that hell hole? He wouldn't be the first.

Jules ran over and stared up at the huge warrior. "Whoa. Are you okay? I didn't hurt you, did I? I was trying to help. I'm new at this."

Zon knelt down on one knee and took Jules's hand in one

of his. "I pledge my fealty to you, Gold Witch. Only say the word and I will serve you above all others. I ask only that you allow me to free my brethren from the pits of hell."

"Oh, uh. Thanks, but I'm all good. I think you have others you need to be, uh, serving, don't you? So go do that freeing your brethren thing."

Zon rose up and released Jules's hand. Which was good because Dax was feeling quite a fit of jealous rage coming on and he didn't want to act like a giant ass. "Cage will want to know of your escape. He's been searching the whole damn world for you and the other Golds who were taken prisoner at The Lindens."

"Yes. I will present the body of the Succubus Queen to him and ask that we mount a full-scale attack to rescue the rest of our brothers." Zon indicated toward the body of the succubus.

They turned back and found that Geshtianna's head and body were no longer lying in pieces on the ground. She was completely gone. Disappeared. "I know I'm learning about new things in the supernatural world and all. But are zombie succubus queens a thing?"

Zon growled, "No. She is dead. I felt her allure over me die when she did." He pointed to scrape marks near where her body had been. "Someone has taken her."

Gal and the two kids were kneeling on the ground around Max. He'd stayed in his wolf form, probably to heal better.

"Hey, dragons. If you're finished saving the world over there. We need to get Max to Doc. Who wants to be our medivac?" Galyna interrupted the new mystery with her fear-filled request.

"I owe my life to you all. I am at your service until Cage arrives and we go back down to Hell for the rest of our Golds. Allow me." Zon shifted and carefully lifted the wolf into one claw and Gal into the other. She pointed him in the direction of Doc's office in town and a gust of wind pushed them skyward without the dragon even having to jostle his passengers with the flapping of his wings.

Jules rushed over to the pickup truck. "Is everyone else okay? The kids?"

Niko gave Dax a small salute, thanking him for what they'd done here on the battlefield today. Kosta and Heli stood together, both on their phones, probably spreading the news through the pack. Selena was just pulling a sweater over her head and it looked as though the last remnants of her injuries were fading to nothing. Dax could not let an attack like this happen again. Geshtianna, the lady in red, may be dead and the immediate threat to the wolf pack children over, but there was clearly a darker plot at work here. He guessed the Black Witch was at its core.

While Jules fussed over her friends, her family really, and they over her and her new powers, Dax called into Cage's command center in Dubai. The phone rang less than once before the gruff male voice answered. Not of Cage, but of Dax's own alpha, the Red Dragon Wyvern, Maciej Cervony.

"Did you see her?" No hello, how you doing, from Match. Nope. All business.

At least he had some good news to share. "Geshtianna is dead, and with the help of one of the missing Gold Dragons."

"Not her. Never mind. I'm on my way. I'll be there tomorrow. Keep your eyes open. This is as close to anyone as she'd gotten since the twins ' birth." Match hung up before Dax could get another question in edgewise.

His phone rang less than a second later. "Cage?"

"Good job, kid. This is the break we needed. Tell the wolves we'll be there tomorrow. Keep them safe until then, will ya?" Cage really did have eyes and ears everywhere. He too hung up before Dax could say another word.

Okay. No pressure. The two most powerful Wyverns in the world were coming to Rogue. He had wanted backup for the wolves. Once more his phone rang. "Hello?"

"Daxy. Daxonian, Dax the max. You should have told me you were in town. How come I had to hear it from Jakob, dude?"

"Sorry. I meant to call you when I got in last night, but it's been a flurry since I got here. I'm glad I got you though. I wanted to ask you--"

"No worries. Fleur and I will be there tomorrow. Oh, hey. Gotta run. Jakob's on the other line." Steele hung up on him too.

What was it with dragons everywhere who didn't want to let him talk? Well he didn't want to talk to them either. He did want to ask Steele about some of the intricacies of when he'd mated Fleur, but it didn't really matter. Regardless of what his friend told him, Dax was going to claim Jules. As soon as possible.

"Hey, dragon." Tristan called to him. He stood leaning against the truck with his hands in his pockets.

"What's up, kid?" Did he look older than ten minutes ago? He was definitely a teenager. That was really weird.

"You should take Jules home. I don't think she feels good." The kid jerked his head in the direction of the group of women left standing at the front of the truck. "That stuff she did took a lot out of her. She's been good to us and we love her. Do you?"

Getting called out by a teenager. Awesome.

Did he, though? He wasn't sure he believed in that concept. Jules was literally the light in his life. He didn't know if she wanted a dragon for a mate, but he knew he wanted her. He'd figure out the love thing later.

He socked the kid in the arm in the long-held tradition of men saying thanks and made his way into the women's group. "Ladies. I think we all need to make our way home and rest. Two Wyverns are on their way here and will be arriving tomorrow. Let's take this time to regroup and recover."

They agreed and Dax shooed the women, except for Jules and the kids into the truck, then shifted. He picked Jules up in his claw and she leaned her head against his leg.

"Dax?" Her voice was soft and sleepy. He couldn't wait to tuck her into bed and curl up with her as she slept. His marking and claiming of her would have to wait until she was rested.

Yes, lass?

She yawned and wrapped her arms around his leg. He tucked his talons around her just a little bit tighter so she wouldn't have to fear falling. He could almost feel her eyes drooping.

"Will you take me to bed?" Her voice was so soft and innocent. She probably had no idea what she'd asked him to do.

He would be a gentleman, he would be a gentleman. If it killed him, death by blue balls, he would be a fucking gentleman. *Aye, love. That's where we're headed. You'll be tucked in and asleep in no time.*

"No. I mean... well, I want you to, uh...unless you don't want... I mean. Grrr." She was adorably flustered.

Dax could hardly dare to believe she was asking him to fuck her. He wanted that more than he wanted his next breath. The connection he felt with her was different than anything he'd ever experienced with any woman and he wanted more. So much more.

Say it, Jules. Tell me what you want from me.

"Take me home and make love to me."

Dax tucked his wings in and a gust of wind propelled them so fast, the air boomed. Either they'd broken the sound barrier flying that fast, or that was the sound of his heart exploding with joy and excitement.

FOREPLAY

*J*ules's fingers shook and she fumbled the key to the front door for the eleventeenth time. Nervous? Yes. Excited? Double yes.

Dax's hand closed over hers and steadied her hand. He brought her fingers up to the lock and pushed the key in with one quick thrust. She swallowed and rolled her eyes at herself. Unlocking a door should not be considered sensual. Keys were not foreplay.

Unless they were being held by Dax. God, he smelled good. She couldn't think of anything else. Except maybe licking him from the divot in his chin to his belly button, and then lower. She was going to spend a lot of time exploring every part of his hard, hot body with her tongue.

She crossed her fingers he wanted to do the same.

Dax pressed his body against her back and his lips to her ear. "Open the door, Jules. If you don't I may take you right here on your tiny front porch in full view of all your very nosy neighbors."

All the flutters of all the butterflies in the universe took a tumbling roller-coaster flight from the bottom of her stomach to the insides of her thighs. She turned that key in the lock so fast it didn't even have a chance to stick like normal. They practically fell into her foyer and Dax kicked the door shut behind them.

Jules did indeed have very nice, but overly-interested-in-her-business neighbors and she was already going to be the talk of the block for having a dragon land in her front lawn. She didn't even care a little bit what they thought. She only cared what Dax was thinking at this moment. Like, should she offer him a drink? Some breakfast? Was it completely out of the question to drag him straight down the hall and ask him to strip while she watched and ran her fingers all up and down that six-pack of abs he was hiding from her under that t-shirt?

"Don't be nervous. I won't do anything you don't want, love. We can take it slow if you want. We'll start with some soft kisses, like this." Dax swept a lock of her hair behind her ear and ran his fingertips along her jaw and over her pulse beating so fast in her throat. Everywhere he touched tingled and heated. He followed his own path with tiny kisses on her cheek, over her chin, and he traced his teeth down her neck.

Those tingles? They turned to flames. "Oooh. I'm not nervous. I don't want to take it slow. I was one-hundred percent wondering if it would be too forward of me to drag you directly to my room and make you strip tease for me."

Dax picked her up under her knees and lifted her into his arms, like she was no bigger than a doll. "Which way?"

He didn't even wait for her to answer. He carried her down the only hall in her small one-bedroom house, kicked open the bathroom door, kept going and found her bedroom in the next doorway. Her very favorite part of the house, and the reason she'd bought it in the first place was the gorgeous little fireplace in the bedroom. She loved having a fire burning there in the evenings, while she read in bed. It was going to be totally romantic if she had half a chance to stop and light it. Maybe later.

She'd decorated her room in yellows and golds which had so much more significance now this morning than it had yesterday. It wasn't overly girly and Dax was going to look just right sprawled across her bed.

Sprawled across her.

Dax set her down and grabbed her around the waist, yanking her body against his. She licked her lips and he groaned. His brought his face down to hers and his tongue peeked out. He licked along the seam of her lips, asking her to open for him. She didn't hesitate and not only allowed him access to her, but pushed her way into his mouth with her tongue too. Their lips and tongues danced and drove the passion she was already feeling for him even higher.

The wood nestled into a small pyramid ready to light burst into a crackling fire behind her. It matched the fire burning in his eyes. "I'd love it if you let me claim you in front of the fire, lass."

Claim her. God that sounded so hot. "Ooh. yes, please."

If he could use his element to set the scene for their love-making, so could she. She imagined that sunny light inside of her and let the wind flow through her hair. Her bedding, including pillows and bedspread went flying into the air, and she concentrated really hard to land them on the floor and not directly in the fireplace.

Pat on the back to herself. If she could do that, she wanted to try something else too. Jules called the wind back up and it fluttered the bottom hem of Dax's shirt. He chuckled and held his arms up over his head. The shirt wiggled its way up over his abs, his chest, then up and over his head and arms.

"That is a handy skill you've learned. Let's see you do it on yourself too. Off with the shirt, Jules. I'm dying to suck and kiss and lick those creamy breasts of yours." He didn't wait for her to use the wind to undress herself. His hands were under the hem and skimming along her sides, his touch stealing the breath from her lungs in all the best ways. Her shirt went to the floor with his and Dax stood there staring at her.

Gulp. She hadn't thought this through very well. Her libido had gotten the best of her instead of that other voice in her head that said a hottie like Dax didn't match well with a plump nobody like her. Jules wrapped her arms across her belly trying to hide the faded stretch marks that came with puberty, donut addiction, and not enough sit-ups.

Maybe they could have sex with their shirts on. But she couldn't avoid taking off her pants and then he was going to see her butt and all her cellulite. Oh God. What had she been thinking?

"I don't know exactly what's going through your head right now, but I can almost see the smoke coming out of your ears. I hope it's because your body is as much on fire for mine as I am for yours." Dax gently grabbed each of her wrists and unfolded her arms, revealing her pudgy tummy.

She was on fire all right. Her face and cheeks were the temperature of the sun. She was swallowing quick, shallow breaths waiting for his reaction, ready to flee to the bathroom to hide her body and embarrassment if she had to.

Dax dropped to his knees in front of her, putting his face flush with her navel. Great googly mooglies. She prayed she didn't have any belly button lint. He pressed a kiss to the left side of her stomach, and then the right. "Don't hide yourself from me, lass. I want to see, and touch, and taste every inch of you."

That sounded both fabulous and horrifying. Every other man she'd been with had been happy enough to have sex under the covers, in the dark. Because it was early morning, light streamed into the room, brighter than she remembered it being before. There was no part of her he wouldn't see when they were naked. No hiding anything from him. "Even the, uh, not very perfect bits? I'd sort of rather you ignore my muffin top, and the jiggly part of my thighs, please. Also, pretend my butt is at least half the size it is. Kay?"

He chuckled and unbuttoned her pants, pulled down the zip, and tugged the legs so they fell halfway down her legs. "Not a chance. I'm going to bury my face between them and I'll need something to hold on to while I make you squirm and beg me to make you come."

"Oh." Could she get over herself enough to let him do all these dirty, exciting things to her? She really wanted to. Why was she being so lame about it? He said he was attracted to her. She should believe him and get down to the fun.

A lifetime of hearing that she was anything but attractive to men held her back.

She'd spent far too long believing she was nothing, nobody, and frankly ... not worth it. But you know what? She wasn't any of those things. She was a freaking witch. She had something inside of her that no one else did. Not only her powers, but a part of her that had awakened last night. That small flame of love she'd held in her mind 's eye was the true power, a part of the real her.

Being able to share something like that with anyone was a little scary. She couldn't imagine showing her true self to just anyone. But Dax wasn't just anyone. When they were together, she felt like someone.

Jules ran her fingers into Dax's hair. "I think that sounds like fun. I like it when you talk dirty to me."

She bit her lip to keep the giggle from escaping. Had she seriously said that? Like out loud?

Yup. She had, and it didn't even sound ridiculous.

"We're just getting started, my lovely lass." Dax slipped her pants down the rest of the way and Jules slipped one foot out and then the other. He threw them over his shoulder and gazed up at her, that fire so bright in his eyes. The pendant around his neck burned just as bright.

The charm she wore with the sun also shined. She couldn't quite remember where she'd gotten it, but it was important to her. Every other stitch of her clothing was coming off, but she'd keep the necklace on.

Dax didn't seem to notice. He worked his way along her hip, kissing and nipping at her skin with his teeth. The tiny stings from his teeth sent shivers up and down her skin. He snagged the edge of her panties between his teeth and yanked them down on one side. If this was going to become a regular thing with them, she was going lingerie shopping.

Oh, please, let there be a next time.

"You should probably stop wearing these around me all together." He ripped through the material with his teeth and then clipped the other side open with the tip of a dragon talon on one hand. They fell to the floor in shreds. "Otherwise you'll probably go through quite a few when I tear them off."

"I'll try to remember that." A tiny, giddy giggle popped out. Dax wanted more too. She felt like clapping, but restrained herself. Barely. Mostly because he buried his face in her thatch of curls and pushed his tongue between her legs and Jules lost all train of thought. She bit her lip to keep from moaning too loudly and sending the neighbors into conniptions.

Dax did wrap his hands around her hips and dug his fingers into the flesh of her butt cheeks. She couldn't get away, even if she wanted to. Which she didn 't. Jules shoved her hands into his hair and ran her fingers over and over his scalp. Good God, he had a talented tongue.

"Dax, oh right there again, please. Don't stop doing that. You feel so good." Jules 's knees tremored, then moved into a full on shake as he pushed her closer to coming. Jeez. He was about a thousand times better than any battery-operated boyfriend she 'd ever had. Where had this dragon been all her life?

He groaned and, with his mouth wrapped around her very center, she didn't understand his mumbling. But whatever he said made her knees go out from under her all together. She was so close to coming in those two tiny minutes. Dax pulled away from her, probably because she was about to fall on top of him. His mouth glistened and he licked his lips.

"Come down here with me. I want you naked and spread out on the blanket so I can feast on every bit of you." He tugged on her hand, but it wasn't like he had to do a whole lot of convincing. He brought her to her knees, so they were facing each other. "I can't wait another minute to do this. "

Dax grabbed her face and took her mouth in a hard, sensuous kiss. His tongue pressed in and out of her lips, and she tasted her essence on him. The carnality of that moment had her whimpering with pure need. There was more to this than a meeting of mouths and tongues. Heat poured into her, not the figurative sexual kind melting her brain, but actual warmth licking at her tongue and throat. He was giving her his fire.

Jules threw her head back and gasped at the feeling of the flames dancing along her insides. It was anything but painful. More like drinking a panty-melting aphrodisiac. It pooled in her belly and warmed her from the inside out. "More Dax, give me more of you, of your fire."

"Fuck, you're beautiful. I can feel you everywhere the flames touch you and I need more." He extended that talon again and snipped her bra in two at the front, then slid it down her arms.

Her breasts were cool where the clothing had covered her skin, keeping the flames away and her nipples pebbled. Dax palmed both, lifting them and caressing the chill away with his fingers. "Look how they overflow my hands. I could get lost in your tits for a lifetime."

He dropped his head and sucked one tip into his mouth and suckled hard. He licked with his tongue and the flames inside his mouth matched the rhythm. The sensation was so intense and he'd built her up so high that she thought she might come just from his mouth on her nipple. "Dax, I want you. Please, I want you inside of me. I need you."

"I'd love nothing better. Except maybe you on top later." Dax waggled his eyebrows all while spreading her legs with his knees. "I'm going to make you feel so good you're going to forget any other man you've ever been with. Starting right here."

Dax pressed his lips to the crook of her neck which did indeed feel absolutely fantastic. Way better than any regular ole necking. His touch sent a strange tingle all through her shoulder and across her chest. "Ooh. Do that again. More."

Dax licked the same spot and nipped at her skin. "Jules. I want to mark you. Show the world that you're mine."

"Mmm-hmm. I don't know what that means, but if a part

of it is doing more of whatever you're doing to my neck right now, I'm in." She wouldn't mind everyone knowing that she was with him.

"Do you want that, to belong to me?" Dax scraped his teeth along the muscle in her neck all the way down to her shoulder.

Holy she-didn't-know-what. Because what he was doing to her was anything but holy, but it sure was like a religious experience. "I like the sound of that. Is this a reciprocal thing? Because that's hot and I really want you to use your teeth on me like that again, but only if it means you're going to belong to me too."

"Oh yes. Yes, it does." Dax licked that same spot again, blew on it, sending shivers across her skin.

Whoa, not just shivers, but fire. That same flame they'd been playing with before circled and spiraled in a pattern along her collarbone, sending pure desire into her. "Do it, Dax. Mark me. Make me yours."

Dax didn't hesitate, he wrapped his arms around her, held her head to the side and chased the flames. He bit down on that spot between her neck and shoulder, not quite breaking the skin, but enough that it would bruise. He sucked hard and sent even more fire into her skin. Even though it should hurt, the very opposite seeped into her. Dax growled deep and gutturally, sending the fire on her skin shooting through her body and straight to her core.

Jules threw her head back as her body convulsed with so much pleasure. She'd been so turned on by him that this last most intimate moment pushed her over the edge into a shattering orgasm, "Oh my, fucking dragon, yes, yes, yes."

Dax reached between their bodies and slid his cock into her wet channel. He made her feel so full, to right. He filled her so perfectly and her body responded to his, clenching him tight inside of her. He slid in and out, slowly, seating himself fully before starting the torture all over again. She lost herself in the feeling of their bodies joining, becoming one.

Not once did he release her skin from the hold he had on it with his mouth and teeth. Not even when his own groans took on the intensity of hers. Jules wrapped her hands around his neck, holding the back of his head in her palms, never wanting him to let go of her. His own control was slipping and he pistoned his hips, driving into her faster now, his rhythm faltering as they got closer to nirvana.

She was so close to coming again and this time, she wanted him with her. She whispered naughty sweet nothings into his ear, hoping to push him over the edge. "You make me feel so good. I'm on fire for you. Make me come again. Give me your fire. Come for me."

He gripped her hips in his hands and pushed into her once, twice, three times more. His body shuddered and he finally opened his mouth, letting go of her shoulder and roared out her name. "Jules, fuck yes, Jules. You are mine. Mine. Mine. Mine."

His words, the pure eroticism of the moment, and the power of his release, sent her soaring into another powerful orgasm. The air was sucked from her lungs as her body erupted into pleasure. Flames flared upon her arms and legs, moving from her skin to his and back in a dance stoked by a fluttering breeze.

The walls and ceiling of her room sparkled and shined in the flickering light of his fire and she matched it with rays of sunshine that poured out of her. Their souls joined and became more than they ever would be on their own. Together, they made magic.

MORE PLAY

$\mathcal{H}$e would never get enough of her. Jules was the spark to his fire, the heat to his flame. Without a doubt, he would never be able to live without her and her love ever again. He didn't know how this was possible, or what it meant, but he was more sure of this one thing than he had been of anything else in his life. Jules was his. Forever.

They would figure out the rest together. Later. After he took her about a dozen and half more times.

His cocked twitched, still buried inside her sweet heat and still he wanted more. He should be completely replete after the most intense orgasm of his life. He should be passed out asleep. They hadn't even caught their breaths from the last climax and all he could think about was pushing her body to give him another orgasm and another.

First he needed to take care of her and her body. Make sure his mark and claim on her hadn't hurt. He'd lost all his control with her. Even his fire had taken on a will of its own. With her stoking it with her wind and letting her sunshine dance with the flames, they could have burned down the whole damn house.

"Lass, are you okay?" He propped himself up on his elbows loving the feeling of her pinned beneath him, but not wanting to squish her. "I didn't hurt you, did I? I'm sorry I lost control for a minute there. You drove me a bit to distraction."

She blew a bright red lock of hair out of her eyes and wrapped her legs around the back of his calves. "That was the hottest part. I loved it. You're damn good in bed, dragon."

Dax grabbed a lock of hair between his fingers. Bright, brilliant red. Not orange like the redheads he usually lusted after, but a beautiful crimson. The color of his scales. "You're the one who is hot in bed. It's never been that intense, nor quite so mind-blowing for me before you. Wasn't your hair brown?"

"Yes, my hair is brown. What were you saying about mind-blowing? Did we break your brain?" She smiled and rubbed her hand across his jaw.

Dax lifted the strand of hair up so she could see the bright color. It was definitely red, but there were streaks of pure shining gold too. Her eyes crossed trying to look at it. "Uh. That's not my hair."

"It's attached to your head. Maybe this is part of your latent powers. I adored your cute brown hair, but this red color is driving me a bit crazy. Do you suppose your hair everywhere turned red?" Oh yeah. He was going there. Dax pulled out of her warm body, begrudging the loss of her heat, but he had to know. He rolled off and threw her legs up in the air and over his shoulders.

"Oh my God. What are you doing, you weirdo." She squirmed and giggled. "I can't see in this position. Are you going to tell me or not?"

"Holy shit, babe. Bright fucking fire-engine red." He was going to spend so much time with his face buried in those curls. His cock went from semi-hard to stone.

"If you call me fire crotch, I'm never sleeping with you again." She shook her finger at him and wrinkled up her nose.

She was so fucking cute. Dax laughed and dove straight into her new fiery curls. She was still wet from their love-making and he lapped at her sensitive little clit, lashing the tip of his tongue over it. He pushed two fingers into her pussy and felt the heat of his own release inside of her. He surprised himself with the thought that he wanted his seed to fill her, to see her belly swollen with his child.

He slid his fingers deeper inside and instead of emulating the action of his cock, he crooked his fingers inside of her and pushed against her inner walls searching for exactly the right spot.

"Dax. God, I don't think I can come again." Her delicious little whimpers and the way her hands went into his hair and kneaded at his scalp contradicted those words.

She would come again. And again. He suckled on her clit, pulling it gently between his lips while tickling her inner walls with his fingers. He knew he found just the right spot when her hips lifted off the floor and she cried out. Then he sucked hard on her clit and lashed at it with his tongue, relentlessly driving her higher and higher. Her channel fluttered and spasmed around his fingers and he reveled in the thought that his seed was being driven deeper inside of her.

Jules's cries became incoherent words and Dax delivered his final coup. He released just one dancing flame from his dragon's fire and let it flicker over her clit and down to his hand. He allowed the warmth of the fire to slide inside of her and quiver as he rubbed her g-spot.

"Dax. Oh, oh. Dax, Dax, Dax." Jules's muscles locked and she screamed his name as the orgasm over took her entire body. She came around his fingers so hard he could feel her muscles clenching, and her clit pulsed and fluttered inside of his mouth. He continued to push her body, pushing to give him every drop of pleasure, drawing her climax out as long as he absolutely could.

She collapsed back to the floor and still her body shook. Dax lifted his head and the sight of her dazzled him. The fire he'd given her sparkled and spun across her skin, undulating to and fro in time to the beat of her body. Not only had she taken his fire, a feat only other wielders of the element could normally do, but she played with it, making it into a more beautiful version of their powers combined.

Dax licked his way up her body, extinguishing the flames as he went until he'd captured them all, and he was looking at the shining new mark he'd made on her collarbone. A fiery red dragon shone there, looking like a living tattoo on her skin. His mark. No man or dragon would ever doubt that she belonged to a dragon, that she belonged to him.

He kissed each of her eyelids, closed still, and then her satisfied smiling lips. The sunshine pendant went nuts on her neck, sparkling and vibrating.

Jules moaned, "You're insatiable. I'm all up for playing with a vibrating toy, but maybe not on my neck."

She reached up to touch the pendant and met Dax's hand doing the same thing. He lifted the pendant and Jules opened her eyes just in time to see it disintegrate in his fingers and turn into sparkling red, blue, green, gold, black, and white jewels. No. Not jewels. Scales. They lifted out of his hand and swirled in a tiny eddy of air. They rose into the sunshine pouring into her room from the window and disappeared into the light.

"That was cool. But why would she give me a necklace and then take it away?" Jules reached into the light as if she could still touch the residual magic instead of only dust motes.

"Who gave you that necklace?" The scales, so brightly colored, could only have come from one dragon. His friend Steele had said when he had a near death experience that he'd seen the First Dragon and the White Witch.

"I'm not sure. I can't seem to bring the memory into focus," Jules gasped. "You don't think it's that lady in red, the succubus queen whosie-what's-her-face, do you?"

He hadn't meant to scare her. He wanted nothing to ever scare her again. Dax moved to lay on the blanket with her and relaxed. He pulled her onto his chest and stroked his hands through her hair. "No. There was nothing evil about it. It drew its light from your magic and called to mine. I think that was a gift from a divine matchmaker."

Jules mimicked Dax's stroking fingers but on his chest. "Like a goddess? Do dragons have a goddess of love?"

"No. We don't worship any gods, not in the sense of a religion. We do revere the First Dragon and his mate, the White Witch. We're dragons because of him, but we can shift between our dragon and human selves because of her gift of love for him and their children. They are the parents of all Dragonkind. The first Wyverns were their children."

Jules at up and stretched. "Huh. I was sure there was some sort of goddess. Super gorgeous curvy mother nature type, creamy tan skin, sort of Middle Eastern looking like Gal, wears all white, flowing robes and all that."

Dax couldn't resist touching her, he was so damn drawn to her. He ran his hand up the side her rib cage, loving her softness. He kept going and circled her breasts, teasing her before moving his hands up to run along his mark on her. "Is that who gave you the necklace?"

"Maybe. I'm not being coy. It's weird, like she's at the periphery of my vision and I can't quite see her." Jules yawned and threw a leg over Dax's.

She seemed completely comfortable in her nakedness now. He'd worried for nothing. He'd never felt more at ease in his life. There was no after-sex weirdness. Just the two of them enjoying being together. "I know the feeling. It may be because we're both exhausted. When's the last time you slept?"

She blinked thinking for a minute. "About twenty-four hours ago. Yesterday, before I met you."

It seemed incredible that he'd met his mate, marked her, and claimed her in the span of a few hours. There was no denying fate once he'd found her. Okay, so he'd tried to deny it at first. He still didn't understand how he could be mated before Match. That's not how it worked. He'd just have to ask his Wyvern when he arrived later today.

Jules yawned again and Dax used that as an excuse to take action. He pulled her into his arms, wrapped the blankets around her and picked her up. When he set her on the bed, he kissed her long and hard, wanting to linger much longer than he should. He reluctantly broke the kiss and took one large step back knowing full well if he didn't, he wouldn't be leaving her bed anytime soon. "Get some sleep now, my pretty mate."

Her eyes flicked back and forth when he called her his mate. It wasn't like he'd talked to her about what marking and claiming really meant. Only in the heat of the moment. Which made him a huge douchecanoe. He mentally prepared a speech. Maybe he should do the human custom of going down on one knee to ask her to be with him forever. Shit.

What if she said no? What if this was nothing but working off a whole lot of battle-fueled adrenaline. He'd done that plenty of times himself. This wasn't one of those times. Sex with Jules meant something.

Then she patted the pillow next to her. "Come sleep with me."

He needed a little time to think of a plan, on how to talk to her about how they were connected now. He'd plan something romantic and woo her not only into his bed, but into his life. Forever. He could definitely use some advice from a more experienced dragon in his Prime. "There's nothing I want more, but my Wyvern, the alpha of the Red Dragons, is on his way here. So is the AllWyvern, Cage. He's the leader of all dragon warriors during this war with the Black Dragon. I need to fly out to meet them and let them know what's happened here."

"Oh." Her eyes dropped and she fiddled with the blanket, scratching and pulling at an invisible spec of nothing. "Okay, then. I understand. I'll see you around, then."

The light in the room faded as if a cloud had passed overhead in the sky. But it was the light from her that had gone dim. Shit. He was fucking this up left and right. "Lass. No. Come here. Let me show you something."

She frowned but allowed him to take her hand and pull her across the room to a small square mirror hung near the door. He kissed her neck, right over her mark and stepped out of the way so she could see. Her eyes went as wide as they could and she gaped at her reflection. Dax bit the inside of his lip to keep from blurting something dumb out. She needed time to process.

Jules reached up and touched the mark, running her fingers along the design of the red dragon. It stretched and writhed under her hand like a pet vying for more attention. "Whoa."

She didn't say more than that and Dax's nerves were jumping around in his chest like cats on caffeine. He had absolutely no idea what she was thinking. Was she mad? Was she freaking out? He was.

Dax took a breath to say something and Jules held up a single finger to shush him. "A. My sex hair is fan-fucking-tastic and I expect you to do this to me every morning because lord knows I can't get it to have this much body."

"Every morning?" That was a good sign. He would resign himself to being her sex-hair stylist if nothing else. The anxiety jumping around inside of him hadn't yet subsided though, because she hadn't acknowledged the mark. His mark.

"Yes, and B. That is the coolest thing I have ever seen in my life. It's so beautiful. It looks just like you. Thank you."

Holy First Dragon, he could breathe again. You're welcome did not seem like the appropriate response here. "It 's only as beautiful as you are, my love. My mark wouldn't look as good on anyone else. It was made for you. Just as I was."

Jules turned and looked up into his eyes. They shimmered and sparkled with a golden light that hadn't been there before. "What do you mean made for me? How could that be, until a couple days ago I was nothing more than a plain human."

"Fate. We were fated to be mates. I don't profess to know how any of this works, because up until earlier this year dragon warriors weren't even sure we could even still have mates at all. Not since the First Dragon and his mate died. Reds are the last holdout, too. I have no idea how I got so lucky to find you."

Dax had heard that some women didn't do great with the whole fate thing. Everyone liked to think they had choices in life and who they loved was a biggie. At the end of the day she could choose not to be with him, but there would never be another for either of them. They would be miserable, but he would abide by her decision.

Although, he would fight for her. She was worth it.

Jules stayed quiet, looking into his eyes, studying the inside of his soul if he had to guess. He should wait and allow her to come to whatever conclusions about their relationship all on her own. He couldn't do it. "So, uh, what do you think? Because I want you to know it doesn't matter even a little bit to me that we just met or that we're riding the high of battle adrenaline or anything else. I am all in, Jules."

She pulled her lips into her mouth, either thinking or trying not to blurt out like he just had. If she didn't say something soon he was going to--

"This is so freaking cool." She jumped up and wrapped her arms around his neck and peppered his face and neck with a thousand little kisses. "I was sure I was doomed to a boring lonely life where I could only watch all the amazing supernatural beings around me live these amazing lives. Now I am one and fate has dived into the fray too and said here's the dragon, man, warrior, sex god, who you get to fall in insta-love with and it's not weird or creepy to him because he feels the same? Hell, yeah I'm all in."

Thank the First Dragon. Dax had every intention to go out and meet up with Match and Cage before they arrived in Rogue, but that was going to have to wait until after he sexed up his lover one more, or seven more times. He grabbed Jules by the waist and swung her around. She squealed and laughed and the sunshine filled the room once again.

Mark her. Claim her. Mate her.

Give her your soul.

The shard at his neck lit up and its hot red light joined her golden beams. Excitement and love burst through his chest, tightening it until he thought his heart would burst. There was one more thing he had to do.

He set Jules down and dropped down onto one knee. Her hands went up covering her mouth and she did an adorable little dance with her feet. Dax grasped the cord his soul shard hung from and lifted it. "Jules, this shard contains a piece of my soul. It was pulled from me by a powerful witch when I came of age and allowed me the power to take my dragon form. It gave me dominion over the element of fire, but its true purpose was to show me the way to my true mate."

Jules nodded and the glimmer of joyful tears glistened in her eyes.

"Will you take my soul and give me yours in return? I am yours for all eternity. Will you be mine?"

She blinked and nodded her head. Suddenly, her throat bobbed and she swallowed. Her mouth turned down into a frown, and fear burst out of her eyes. "No. No no no no no."

She reached out for Dax, but her arm froze in mid air. Jules 's body went rigid and she collapsed into convulsions.

*D*amn. Damn. Damn.

This vision stuff was getting old real fast. She had the love of a lifetime to get back to and was really looking forward to more fiery orgasms with him. But no. She had to be pulled into another vision. She looked around trying to figure out who or what was interfering with her sex life.

This vision wasn't as foggy or stifling as the previous ones. She'd always been frozen and unable to do anything but watch what was happening around her before. This time she could move, walk about, and interact with whereever she was. This was less a vision and more like she'd been transported somewhere else.

The only reason she was sure her body was still in the bedroom of her little house with the dragon that she loved was the steady heartbeat pulsing from her hands. That wasn't her heart. Dax must be freaking out and at the same time doing all he could to keep her grounded. If they were being forced to be apart right at this critical time in their relationship, she was damn well going to make the best of the situation. The sooner she could get back to him, the better.

"Hello? Is anyone here? What is it you want me to see?" Where before the visions had all taken place outside, this one was somewhere dark and hot. Maybe underground even. Jules reached out and touched the wall of what looked like a cave. The stone was craggy with sharp bits and her hand came away blackened as if everything was covered in soot. Gross.

Up ahead a soft red glow emanated from some sort of larger space than the tunnel she seemed to be in. The color reminded her of the light from Dax's soul shard. The one he had been about to give her.

Jules touched her neck and found the cord and pendant hanging there. Its warmth gave her a modicum of strength and even in this strange state, Dax's love and protection swirled around her. He may not be here with her, but he was still watching out for her. She used that knowledge to give her the courage she needed to move toward the glow and find out what in the world was happening.

At the entrance to the cavern, Jules paused and snuck a quick peek around the corner of the wall. There was indeed a room with half a dozen other tunnels breaking off from this main hub. Nooks were carved into the stone in several places around the room and above each one hung bright sparkling charms of some sort. In fact, they looked like Christmas ornaments. How strange.

She didn't see anyone in the room so it seemed safe enough to venture out and explore. There had to be a reason she was here specifically. The first carved-out area looked like an armory of sorts. There were a lot of very shiny swords, a box covered in small glittering mirrors, and a few armor-type items made of dark red and black leather. It was way too hot down here to be wearing that kind of clothing.

She didn't exactly know what she was looking for, so simply catalogued the stuff in her mind and moved to the next alcove. This one had a platform of some sort carved into the stone. A bed maybe? She glanced across to the other one and saw the same. Sparks moved up and down the entrance to the little alcoves and Jules realized it was a force field of some sort. She didn't see any sort of electrical panel or anything so it must be magical and not futuristic science. Whatever it was, she couldn't see beyond it except for the stone inside.

Handy spell, that. She wouldn't mind learning how to only allow people to see what she wanted them, too. If this was only a vision she could maybe move through the magical force field and see what lay inside. She crept closer and touched just the very tippy tip of her finger to one of the sparks running down from the ceiling. Nothing happened.

Cool. She pushed her hand through and since there didn't seem to be any side effects, stepped through and into the tiny room.

"I see he's captured you. I'd hoped you would become my ally and not my enemy, Gold Witch."

A shot of adrenaline hit her straight in the heart along with a boulder of dread dropping into her gut. A woman dressed in red leather, with about a dozen knives and daggers strapped to her legs, arms, and waist stood against one wall of the cave. On the bed of stone, the image of Ellie, but once again older, lay snuggled up with a stuffed bear sans head. She was both here and in her own bed.

Right before her eyes Ellie's body and face transformed from that of a young teenage girl at that all legs and arms awkward stage into a beautiful young woman. In a couple of blinks of an eye, she aged at least five or six years.

Jules jumped toward the shadowy figure of the girl she'd known as a baby only a day ago. "Stop. What are you doing to her?"

The woman in red shoved Jules so that she fell to the floor and the sharp stone suddenly felt all too real. Her hands stung with the burn of the rock scraping her skin open and she was going to have one mega bruise on her butt when she got out of here.

"I'm saving her from a fate like yours. It's either this," the woman pointed to Ellie, "or this. A red ball of light, formed in the woman's hands, looking more like a colorful crystal ball, rather than a weapon. She threw the fiery orb at Jules's face.

Jules ducked and covered her face with her bleeding hands. The ball struck her anyway and her world flashed into another vision. This one was like the others. She couldn't move, couldn't interact, couldn't breathe. All she could do was stare at the death and destruction around her.

The ground appeared scorched and dead, covered in great patches of slimy black oil and ash. In the sky above her, an army of dragon warriors flew like airplanes, diving and spinning, fighting an army of red-eyed black dragons. One by one the dragon warriors fell to the burnt land all around her. Land that she recognized.

Over there was the strip mall where she'd gotten her first job at a frozen yogurt shop. On the corner was the shell of a gas station still burning. Down the street, where the library should be, was nothing but a great crater in the land. Slowly her body turned, allowing her to see the ruins of Rogue all around her.

Her vision flashed again and she was at the beach. The

bodies of great blue dragons and dozens of dark-skinned mermaids floated in the surf like bodies of soldiers at Normandy. The water was red with their blood.

Her vision flashed and she saw the clearing in the forested reserve where the wolf pack held the mating ceremonies.

The wolves were all there. All of her friends. Dead.

She flashed once more but not far. She floated above the land near the dragon tree that had been created in the last battle the wolves and dragons had against the King of Hell. Below her a group of dragons and women stood together, elemental magic circling and floating all around them. There were two big green dragons, three gold ones, a blue one and two reds. One she recognized.

It was Dax. Oh my God. Dax.

Inside her head she begged, not knowing if the woman in red could hear her or even cared. "Please take me closer. That's my mate down there. I need to see what's happening. Please."

She drifted down and hovered just above the group of dragons standing in a battle against a huge angry black dragon. In one of the claws of the black dragon was the broken body of a man with black and red scales over his body, like he'd died in the middle of shifting.

Beside the Black Dragon, a darkly evil black witch cradled a child in her arms. Her hands and face were bathed in a sparkling silver fluid. It dripped from her mouth in sickly streaks and down her throat where a single white swirled bone hung on a cord. Not a bone, a horn. A unicorn's horn.

The last stand of dragons used their elements together to fight his power and they were losing. The Black Dragon stalked closer, shooting his fire in a steady stream pushing the combined magic of the dragons back with each step.

There weren't only dragons there. In front of each one stood a woman with elemental magic swirling around her, concentrated from the necklaces they each wore at their necks. Soul shards. Jules recognized the colors of the four elements, controlled by witches like her. Dragon daughters. A Green Witch, a Blue Witch, A Gold Witch, and the Red Witch.

There were three more women, though. Two with black tendrils of magic that Jules thought at first was bad. But the magic was shadowy, not evil. They worked in tandem, their magic swirled around creating shadows that protected the others from demons who attacked from the sides. The last woman had a very powerful magic that pulled on each of the others to combine them into a brilliant white light that formed a shield in front of them all.

The women weren't battling the black dragon or the witch, they were protecting their dragons as they fought against this ultimate evil.

Jules's vision allowed her to drift even closer and she landed in the body of one of the women. Her vision self joined with her actual body. She was the woman with the gold elemental magic. She stood in front of Dax, who was bloodied and on the verge of collapse. The shard at her throat flickered, its light fading and faltering.

This couldn't be. She couldn't allow this to be the future. Jules turned her head and found the woman in red standing next to her, tendrils of red fiery magic swirling around her and a huge red dragon. She wasn't a mere woman. She was the Red Witch.

"I can stop this from happening, Gold Witch."

"Then do it. Do whatever you have to. You can't let everyone be killed and their evil take over the land."

"I'm so tired. I can't keep running and hiding. He hunts me

day and night. If I fall, before I can bring the sacrifice and savior the power, this is our future. Help me."

"Who? How? I don't understand." The Red Witch made it sound as if the sacrifice and the savior were people, or maybe dragons or witches.

"Give these to Ellie and Izzy. Do not allow the Gold Dragon to know. He will try to stop you." The Red Witch pressed two small packages into Jules's hand.

"What are they?" The vision wouldn't allow her to see what she held. It looked like nothing but blobs of gold light.

Another surge of fire from the Black Dragon struck at them and the Red Witch's magic splintered fell to her knees. "A gift from the Mother."

"Wait. I don't know anyone named Izzy or her mom."

"Not that mother. Her." The Red Witch looked up and then collapsed to the ground. Her form faded into a pool of red swirling light. The big red dragon behind her roared and charged forward, breaking the line of dragons and the protective barrier the witches were holding between them all and total destruction. Dax, bound to the other red dragon, followed behind him. Both were struck by fire from the Black Dragon, but the fire was tainted with the Black Witch's dark magic. Dax, her Dax, was struck to the ground and his form flickered. He was a man again, and he reached out for Jules with his dying breath.

Pain and terror tore through her as the shard she wore at her neck exploded into a thousand tiny sharp daggers, tearing her apart from the soul up. His body turned to black ash before her eyes and he disintegrated, blowing away in the wind. "Dax, no. Oh god, please no."

Jules screamed and looked up into the sky, wanting to lash out at anything she could. Time froze. A white light, not unlike the that from the White Witch fighting beside them here and now, floated above the battle. Behind the light a rainbow dragon hovered in the air. "The goddess."

If she was a mother and an all-powerful being why didn't she stop this from happening?

Blackness and fire swirled over Jules's vision and the scene in front of her faded. For a brief moment she saw the inside of the stone cave again, but it was empty. No Red Witch, no Ellie, no daggers, no Christmas ornaments. That scene too faded and her own bedroom came into focus.

"Jules? Baby? Thank the First Dragon, you're back." Dax pressed a kiss to her forehead and grabbed her into a tight hug. "I thought I lost you that time. You weren't breathing and your light faded away. I didn't know what else to do."

She grabbed him back just as tight. Tears laced her face and the wail that he had died was on her lips. She buried her face in his chest and sobbed.

"It's okay. You're safe. It's okay. I think my soul shard helped anchor you. Did you feel it in your vision?" Dax petted her hair and hushed her until her tears subsided and she could face the world again. She absolutely could not let the future the Red Witch had shown her happen. She had to do everything in her power to help in anyway that she could.

A face she didn't recognize popped in front of her and examined her with narrowed eyes. "She's back now and hopefully she can tell us how to save the children. Is that what you saw in your vision, young witch?"

Jules screamed and scrambled for the blanket. "What are you doing in my room? Turn around right now. No one but Dax gets to see my girly bits."

"It's okay, lass. No one is seeing any part of you they shouldn't. You're fully clothed. This is Cage Gylden, the

AllWyvern of the Dragon Warriors." He indicated to the man and then pointed to another darker figure standing against the wall next to the fireplace. "And this is Maciej Cervony, my alpha and the Red Dragon Wyvern."

Gulp. Red Dragon.

Jules squeezed her hand tight. The packages the Red Witch had given her were still there. Strange magic indeed. She could not let these two dragon warriors, Wyverns, whatever see that she had them or what she intended to do with them. She didn't understand why they would want to stop her from giving the necklaces... oh, that's what they were, just like the one someone had given to her.

Ellie and Izzy. These necklaces were going to help their mates find them. She couldn't figure out why these two men would want to stop that from happening. She certainly wasn't going to ask though. She wasn't even sure she should bring it up with Dax, especially if these guys were his dragon bosses.

She hated keeping a secret from him, but she would if it meant saving the world. "Get out. Both of you. You're in my room, in my house and I want you out."

"Uh, babe. These are--"

"I don't care if you're the Pope. Go wait in the living room. Now." Jules pulled power from her innermost self and blew a giant gust of wind at the two men, picking them both up and tossing them out of her bedroom door. She heard a very satisfying thunk, thunk as they hit the wall in the hallway and smiled to herself.

"Never let it be said that my mate couldn't hold her own against two of the most powerful dragons in the history of the world." Dax sounded a little shock and awed.

The two Wyverns grumbled out in the hall, but the sound of their voices receded as they moved toward the living room.

"We gotta go." Jules jumped out of the bed and found that Dax had put her into a yellow summery dress she'd never quite had the courage to wear because it was low cut on top and showed off her thighs. This would totally work for saving the world. She shoved the necklaces into the tight bodice of the dress. Next time she was buying a dress with pockets.

Bless Dax for not even questioning her. "Okay. Do you want to head back over to Doc's office where Max is recovering? That's where everyone is. They're freaking out that the kids are so changed. Although we can hardly call them children anymore. Max said Tristan is as tall as he is. Gal's best guess is that they're almost twenty years old-ish."

"I know what to do. Come on." They weren't going to get past two surly dragon dudes. Jules threw open the window and mentally measured to see if her butt and Dax's shoulders were going to fit through the space. Probably. Maybe. Worth a try. "Give me a boost."

Dax lifted her by the waist and set her sideways on the window sill. She scooted over, which hiked the skirt of the dress halfway up. Dax's eyes followed the dress's movement like it was the most fascinating sight in the world. "Is that what you saw in your vision? I think the front door is a better choice, lass. Although I am enjoying seeing your bare ass."

What a time for him to mention that he had clothed her, but had not provided undergarments. Well, he had said not to wear them around him. She got one leg out and half rolled, half fell out the window. She stood up and brushed the dirt off her. "Sort of and no, we need to sneak away from your bosses. I'll tell you why later. Do you know someone named Izzy?"

Dax hopped up, grabbed the frame of the window and slid out easy peasy. "That's Cage's daughter's name."

Of course it was.

UP TO NO GOOD

$\mathcal{H}$is luscious mate was up to something and Dax didn't like it one bit. She shushed him and crept away from her house, bending low so no one would see them out her windows. While that gave him a great view of her ass, he didn't understand why they had to resort to subterfuge around Cage and Match.

Jules stopped when the reached the farthest corner of the house from her living room where the Wyverns were waiting. "We'll get there faster if you fly us. But keep it on the down low, I don't want your dragon friends following us. I don't trust them."

Oh shit. "Then trust me. They are here to help."

"I'm sorry. I know they're your bosses or whatever, but I need to do something and I don't want them to interfere. Please, Dax. Take me to Doc's. I need to find Ellie right away."

Dragon warriors didn't interfere. They protected and served. Dragon warriors saved the world on a daily basis. Her visions had steered them in the right direction so far, but they weren't perfect. She could have misinterpreted this last one if it told her to avoid the dragon warriors. "This has to do with your vision? The one that almost killed you? Tell me. We can create a plan of action together."

"Yes, I know what to do because of the vision. I can't say more than that now except the other dragons can't get in the way."

Dax studied her, looking for clues in her eyes as to what had happened to make her distrust the men who could help them the most. Yes, he was also stalling. He needed a minute to process what she was thinking and what he was going to do about it. He couldn't avoid other dragons his entire life. He needed to both protect her and do his duty to the world keeping everyone safe from the hellish plague that was the Black Dragon and his minions. She knew that. Which made it all the more confusing that she was asking him to essentially escape from the purview of the Wyvern. He had to trust her if he expected the same in return. He'd figure out her agenda and a way to allow the dragons to help. He kissed her quickly and shifted.

Jules climbed into his claw for the ride over to Doc's office. He told himself over and over that he was doing the right thing. It didn't help. He still felt like a total piece of shit, because the second he'd shifted, he called to Match.

Jules has asked me to take her to the wolves. Meet us there and bring every man, woman, wolf, and dragon. She has yet to tell me what's going on.

Match grunted before answering. *Your ... woman clearly wants nothing to do with any other dragons, little brother.*

I know. Her last vision was different than the others and it almost killed her.

He was doing the right thing. He had to keep telling himself that. The instant he shifted, Match and Cage had known. It wasn't like he could hide from them. They were the alphas. But he didn't have to tell them where they were going. Neither of the Wyverns had used the command ingrained into their alpha's voices to compel him to say anything. He'd volunteered that information and in doing so betrayed his mate.

Lass, we need to call in my brethren. They will help us.

"No, I know what to do. We just need to find Ellie and Izzy. We don't need them for anything. I promise."

She was going to find out in the next ten minutes that he'd already made that call because every dragon in or near Rogue was going to be at Doc's office by the time he and Jules arrived. A tight ball of self-loathing pulled at his chest, making it hard to breathe.

He'd only just convinced Jules they belonged together and here he was giving her a reason to not want to be with him. He hated what he was doing and yet would do it all over again. Because he couldn't protect Jules on his own. Her last vision had ground that into his brain. She'd almost died and he could do nothing but lay his soul shard around her neck and pray to the First Dragon that his small action would do something, anything to help her.

She had come back to him. With a plan. That she wouldn't tell him about.

Trust her. He was doing the right thing. Which was it?

The small clinic for supernatural beings that Doc ran came into view and Dax circled, nice and slow, down into a landing. He 'd taken as much of their sweet time as he could get away with. Cage had the power of the wind on his side to propel him and Match here much faster. Eventually, he 'd love someone to teach Jules how to use her power that way too, but right now he was damn glad she was new at wielding her control over her element.

Jules was out of his claw and running toward the entrance before they even hit the ground. Crap. He hoped she wasn't met with a wall of dragon warriors and that she wasn't going to kick his ass if she was.

Both of those things were probably going to happen. Fuck a duck. And this day had started out so well.

Dax shifted and jogged into the clinic behind Jules. The wall of dragon warriors was definitely there and Jules was on fire. Not literally, but she might as well have been with the way the sunshine poured out of her and the wind whipped through her hair. She looked just like that little girl in the *Firestarter* movie.

"Lass, I'm--" His words were cut off by a fireball aimed straight at his head. He ducked, but not in time. The bomb was going to hit him straight on. Jules waved her hand and a gust of wind lifted the ball up over his head and out the front door where it landed in a garbage can. Maybe she knew how to use her magic better than he 'd thought. He didn 't know if that was good or bad right now.

A woman with long black hair, holding the sword of the Gold Wyvern, and dressed in red leather conjured another ball of fire. "Stay back, dragon. She's already fallen to you, but I need her now."

Match stepped between the woman in red and Dax. He called forth his own fire, in a show of power equal to hers. "Fallyn, Stop. You know he isn't going to harm her."

Fallyn? Holy shit on a single shingle. The woman or witch or whatever Match had been hunting since she'd tried to kill him down in Hell was standing here in the clinic ready to wreak havoc on them all. What a fool he'd been to think

Geshtianna had been the woman in red the children had been telling them about. Even the Succubus Queen didn't have the power to make the babies grow into adults practically overnight. Only a very powerful witch, one who dealt in dark magic, could do something like that.

No way was he allowing that woman anywhere near his mate. If anything proved to his Jules that the dragons were on her side, this should be it. Dax darted around Match's back and toward his mate. He didn't exactly have a plan except to get her out of harm 's way, away from this fire witch.

He raced toward Jules, ready to shift if he had to. Mid-step, he was lifted into the air the same as that fireball. He floated up to the ceiling and got his first good look at what was really going on. Jules had Cage pinned in the air as well and the AllWyvern was fucking livid. His face and growl distinctly communicated that Dax had better do something.

Dax called upon his dragon. He 'd just sit on them with his big dragon ass, pin them to the ground. He couldn't imagine why no one else had thought of that. Scales flittered across his skin, but wouldn't come forth. Something was blocking his shift. He glared at the red witch. It had to be her.

"Jules, love. Let us down, we can help you. I'll protect you. I promise these dragons are no threat to you." His shard around her neck glowed brightly with each of his words. He could practically feel her love for him pouring out of her and into him through that small piece of himself he'd given to her.

Tears bubbled up over her lashes and streamed down her face. "You don't understand. I have to help her."

"What? No. Lass. Listen to me." Help the witch? That couldn't be right.

Galyna burst through the door that led to the back where Doc had hospital beds and such set up. "Ellie is missing."

She took in the scene, skidded to a stop, gasped, and backed away from the standoff. She didn't get far because a gorgeous black woman stepped out behind her blocking her escape route. Azy. Cage's mate and the mother of the first-born dragon babies of their generation. "So is Apollo."

Cage roared and his dragon flashed in his face and scales shimmered across his skin. "Let me down, witches, and tell me what you've done with my son."

Jules pushed him farther away and glanced over at Fallyn, who nodded at her. Whatever their communication meant, it showed Dax exactly whose side Jules was on, and it wasn't his. The heart that had just a few hours ago felt invincible and filled with the light and warmth of love went cold and crumbled to dust. He struggled for breath as his body adjusted to the gaping maw in his chest where his heart had been.

She'd tricked him. Very convincingly. He'd known all along that she wasn't his mate. No dragon could find his until their Wyvern found, marked, claimed, and mated their own true love. Match was one cranky son of a bitch who had dedicated his entire life to fighting the demon wyrms. He didn't have time or even care about finding a mate.

No Red Dragon Warrior should. They were here to save the world, not play house with pretty plump witches who rocked their worlds so hard they forgot their missions and their heads. He was such a dumb ass.

He'd been sent to Rogue and the Troikas to protect them and instead of nullifying the threat, he'd bedded her. He should have his warrior card revoked. His cock had just doomed them all.

He was never using it ever again. Then he could be a cranky old man like Match. At least then they'd all be safe instead of bringing on the destruction of the world.

Fallyn looked up at Cage and then pointed to Match. She lit a circle of fire all around him, but this one burned not just with their shared element, but with a sparkling magic that brought the Red Wyvern to his knees. She pointed to him and said, "Not yet."

Match roared in anguish and the fires around him burned hotter and brighter. Fallyn frowned and rubbed at her forehead. "Shut up, all of you. I'm fighting for us all. Shut. Up."

Cray-cray was having a moment and that was Dax's chance to do something. He pulled his fire up from deep inside and opened his mouth to shoot it at the two witches. He coughed and choked on his own flames. He couldn't do it. He could not harm Jules. Fuck.

It had to be because she was wearing his soul shard. He had to get it back. He vowed he would take possession and never give it to any woman ever again.

"Hey, bitch-face. I thought we were friends. I helped you. I let you hold my baby. We named our daughter Isolda because of you. The whole damn Wyr calls her Izzy. What the hell is going on now? Did you kidnap my son?" Azy ground her fist into her hand and moved toward Fallyn and Jules. If anyone could hold their own against two witches it was a half-mermaid half-badass from the south side of Chicago.

"Yeah, get her Azy," Dax shouted.

Cage threw a death glare at him, but joined in from the peanut gallery on the ceiling. "Yes, love of my life. Kick her ass."

Jules lifted their would-be attacker into the air and brought her up next to Cage. She scowled at Azy. "You should be helping us. Aren't you the Blue Witch?"

"Who you calling witch, witch?" Azy swung her arms and

legs trying to kick or punch or maybe air swim at Jules. It didn't work.

"She doesn't know. I had too many voices in my head back then. I didn't know or I did and I didn't." Fallyn shook her head and pain was evident on her face. Her crazy was showing in the furrows on her brow. "We need her. We need them all. Where are the shadows?"

Azy sighed and shook her head. "Fallyn, you're not making any sense. Let us all down and we can help you. You know me. I'm your friend. But I won't be if you hurt my kids or my mate. Do you hear me?"

"We have to go. One of the shadows is already battling Ereshkigal. The end is nigh." Fallyn pointed at Cage. "The Golds are under the tree. Quit dicking around and get them out. Their light is giving me a headache."

"What tree? I don't understand, you insane piece of hell." Cage grabbed Azy's hand and his scales shimmered again. For the first time since Jules had pinned them to the ceiling with her power of the wind, Cage's own element fought against her. She must be getting tired, using her magic in such a long-sustained burst like this. The wind whipped around her hair and got in her face. She blew at it and spit it out, but it was enough of a distraction that Cage and Azy floated to the floor.

Fallyn grunted in frustration. "The dragon tree. Pay attention. Save them and the winter shadow. I can only do so much by myself. I'm tired."

Cage growled. "What about Apollo? If we save them and this winter shadow, will you return him to us?"

Fallyn shook her head and sighed like the AllWyvern was not the brightest star in the sky. "I don't have him."

Azy went ballistic. "Don't be cryptic with me. I want my son back."

Dax could hardly wait for Azy to figure out how to get down from here and beat Fallyn senseless.

"He's not yours anymore." Fallyn actually sounded sort of sad when she said that. This was one crazy lady. Dax guessed being raised in hell by the Black Dragon would do that to a person.

Azy didn't like that answer at all. "Yes. He. Is."

Fallyn shrugged. "Not for long. We have to go. Now." She reached into her vest and brought out a mirror.

"You stole my mother's mirror, too? We need to have a talk about right and wrong. Come here and I'll let my fist introduce you to the concept of do-the-right-thing." Azy was practically vibrating with anger. Water pooled around her feet and if it didn't smell like the sea, Dax might have thought she peed from being so fucking pissed off.

"Save your power. You're going to need it. Soon." Fallyn pointed the sword she'd taken from Cage at Jules.

Dax's fire flared and his dragon roared to the surface. That was his mate and nobody was going to kill her. Except him. Damn it. The wind that had been holding him to the ceiling released him and he dropped to the floor. He stalked toward his wayward mate. Fallyn stabbed her right through the heart and she cried out. Before his very eyes, she disappeared. That hole in his chest was nothing compared to the emptiness eating him from the inside out. Pain rippled out from his breastbone and made his entire rib cage ache.

Fallyn pointed the sword at her own chest, stabbed herself Juliet style, and she was gone, too. Good riddance.

Match howled with a pain that equalled the way Dax felt right now. He rushed to his Wyvern's side and tested the fires surrounding him. They should both be able to control the flames and certainly shouldn't be hurt by them. Dax reached into the fire and real pain like a thousand daggers piercing his flesh made him pull away. Fucking dark magic.

How Match endured it for as long as he had spoke to the pure strength and power of the Red Wyvern. Sweat, actual beads of perspiration broke out on his temples and poured down the side of his face. Match groaned and looked up at Dax. "Go after her. Save her."

"What? No. First we're saving your ass. Then we're hunting those witches down." There was no saving the woman he'd thought was his mate. There was no saving his own soul. "Azy, can you use some of that water to douse the flames?"

"I'll try. I'm not great with the water when I'm not in it." Raindrops fell from the ceiling, but the fire burned so hot they evaporated before they reached Match or the flames themselves. "Sorry. Let me try something else."

Azy continued to throw different water features at Match and none of them had any effect. They needed to figure out something else.

"Listen, Daxton Cervony." The power of Match's alpha voice resonated through Dax's brain.

Whatever his Wyvern was about to tell him to do, he would not be able to refuse. Whatever it was, he would do it. He was ready to sacrifice himself in Match's place if needs be. The pain of the witch's fire would be a welcome feeling. Then maybe he could ignore the pain around where his heart used to be.

"I'm listening. What would you have me do?" If he was lucky Match would ask him to burn down hell. That sounded like a great fucking idea.

Match grunted in pain and his breathing labored to come out. His words were harsh and guttural. "Save. Your. Mate."

He'd do anything. But he couldn't do that. "I'm sorry, sir. I... I can't. She's not my mate. She can't be. I thought we were something special. That the First Dragon and the White Witch had made a mistake and given her to me before you found your mate. I'm sorry everyone had to see what a dumbass I am."

Azy found the clinic 's fire extinguisher and shot it straight at Match 's chest. He breathed out a sigh of relief. Azy emptied the canister on him. The fire wasn't gone, but Match stood and grabbed his own sword from his scabbard. He thrust it through the torturous flames and into Dax 's hands. "Take this, you 're going to need it. And you are a dumbass. But not for thinking you couldn't have a mate. That falls on my shoulders. It is clear to us all that she is yours."

The power of the Red Wyvern 's sword poured into Dax. He felt like he could do almost anything. "But how? You haven't even found yours, much less marked, claimed, or mated her."

Match sighed, looked over at Cage and then back to Dax. "But I have."

Cage threw his hands up in the air. "What? Who? When? Why haven't you presented her to the AllWyr?"

"Because, brother, you know as well as I that I haven't been able to catch her. Every time I do find her, she tries to kill me." Match pointed to the spot where Fallyn had stood only moments before. "She reviles and fears me above all others."

No. He couldn't mean Fallyn. Evil incarnate ... mated to the Red Wyvern. He had a bad feeling about this.

Match grabbed Dax 's arm through the flames, even though they had to be torture. "Don't let the same thing happen to your mate. Save her."

CRAZY IS AS CRAZY DOES

"What in hell is going on?" Jules sucked in the hot air and pulled out a ball of sunshine so she could see where Fallyn had taken them. She wasn't entirely sure she wasn't dead. The witch had stabbed her in the chest. Although it didn 't hurt. Instead her head had gone all fuzzy and then she was stumbling around in the dark until Fallyn appeared in the same place.

"This is only the edge of hell." Fallyn looked around the darkness and then headed down a tunnel Jules hadn't even seen. "We have a ways to go to get to actual hell. So we need to hurry."

Nope. This was not working out the way she had hoped. But really what did she think was going to happen when she betrayed the love of a good man-dragon-warrior trying to save his and everyone else 's life? That it was going to be easy peasy lemon squeezy? That was not how life worked. Not hers anyway. "I'm not going anywhere else with you until you tell me exactly who you are and what is going on. I just left my mate back there and he thinks I've betrayed him."

Fallyn stalked back to her and got right up into her face. "You remember what I showed you, don 't you?"

Jules shivered despite the heat and nodded. "Yes, of course."

"Then you know who I am and what we 're trying to prevent. We have to get that necklace to the girl." She crossed her arms and her eyes. "I'd hoped you had already done it."

"Sorry." Jules resisted drawing the word out like a third grader, but barely. "I went straight to where I thought she was when I woke up."

"We 're wasting time talking about this. You weren't fast enough. End of story. Now we have to save her and her dragon, too." Fallyn marched away, obviously expecting Jules to follow her.

She did. What else was she supposed to do? She had no idea where she was and the sunshine she held onto was fading fast. She didn 't really understand how it worked, but figured she needed to refill herself in actual sunlight. Kind of like Superman. Yeah. Cause she was a superhero. Not. She rolled her eyes at herself and hurried to catch up to Fallyn. The only light she had now was the glow from Dax 's soul shard. "What do you mean her dragon?"

"You ask too many questions. Use your powers to see the answers and let 's get a move on. Ereshkigal is not the best mother. She's an even worse witch and nobody will want that boy if she draws his soul out. Then we're all screwed." Fallyn took another turn down a side tunnel and the floor took a steep dip downward.

Jules allowed herself one whole second to let her jaw hang open and to shake her head. So many whats and not enough answers. She scrambled after Fallyn, not wanting to lose her in the darkness. "It's not like I'm psychic."

"Of course you are. Why do you think you've been seeing the future? Duh. You simply needed a little jump start. The Mother didn't have you raised properly. I figured I could kill two birds with one other bird."

"I don't think that's how that saying goes." This lady really was batty. A niggle of worry burrowed into Jules's brain that she'd chosen the wrong team. She 'd seemed a lot more sane in the vision. Now, not so much. Didn't people say that evil villains always thought they were doing bad things because they thought they justified or something? Fallyn could very well be leading Jules to her death because she thought she was supposed to in order to save the world.

Crazy is as crazy does. Including spelunking in hell. She didn't have much of choice now. She'd chosen this dark path and she was going to follow it until she either saved the world and got Dax back or ... no, she did not want to think about that. She really needed to concentrate on not falling and knocking herself out on this uneven terrain. They climbed over boulders and past huge caverns that looked like they housed armies of bats or more likely demons, but were empty.

"I'm new to the whole talking-to-real-people thing. Trust me, it's better that you didn 't access your abilities sooner. The dragons would have probably taken you a long time ago if you had. Bastards. You 're the first of the fallen I've interacted with, but I didn't really have any other choice. Even the winter shadow is tainted. You two are the last of the dragon daughters and I couldn't exactly get to the shadow."

"I only understand about half of what you say." They paused at the sound of shouts and a rumbling up ahead. Someone was fighting a battle down here. That had to be where they were headed. Jules pushed forward, but Fallyn stopped her and backtracked, choosing a different tunnel for them to go down. This one was steeper than the last.

"Huh. Well, I don 't really get you, either. Why would you let that dragon do all those weird things to you with his mouth. It looks gross but all you fallen do it. A lot. Does it placate their beasts or something? Is that why you smash your mouths together?"

Oh God. Was she seriously asking about her sex life? Geez. No one could see her blush so far underground, but her face didn't care and did it anyway thinking about whether had Fallyn seen the dirty things she and Dax had done together. The questions were phrased very strangely though. Like Fallyn had never gotten the birds and the bees talk from anyone. "Umm. Do you mean kissing?"

"Kss, kss, kss." Fallyn repeated the sound over and over like she was testing it. "I think I preferred the biting. That at least I understood."

Biting. Understood. As in the past tense. Jules reached up and touched the place where Dax 's mark was tattooed on her skin. She could feel it moving under her fingers. She knew it meant she belonged to him and even if he never wanted anything to do with her again after this, she would wear it with pride.

"So, uh, did a dragon warrior bite you, Fallyn?" If one had, where was he? Had Fallyn killed him? Jules had absolutely no idea if she'd chosen to ally herself with a good guy or a bad guy. Too late now.

"Shh." Fallyn crouched at the entrance to another split in the tunnel. She waved her hand up and down showing Jules the red sparkles of her magical force field already in place. "We're here. Get ready to put the necklace on Ellie, as fast as you can."

Jules took out one of the packages from her bodice, somehow knowing it was the right one for Ellie. She slid the necklace out and grasped the charm in her hand. The metal circle had half a sun on one side and a partial moon on the other in an almost yin-yang shape. The sun glowed with a golden light similar to her own sunshine and the moon had an almost translucent blue-ish shimmer to it. "I'm ready. What happens then?"

"She'll be marked as a dragon daughter and her dragon can find her and they can save the future. Half of it anyway. Izzy will have to do the rest."

Not exactly the answer she was looking for. What she really needed to know was how they were going to get out of Hell. "But Ellie is the daughter of wolf shifters. She 's not a dragon."

Fallyn made a face like Jules was being really dumb. "You seriously ask too many questions when the answers are right there. There is no such thing as a female dragon. Dragon daughters are not born to dragons. They are made by the White Witch. How did you think you became one and got your powers? By accident? Didn't she tell you? She's bad at that. Not really much better of a mother than her sister."

Finally a small piece she understood. "You're talking about the goddess. Who is her sister?"

"Just do your job, Gold Witch." Fallyn shoved Jules around the corner and into a huge cavern.

Jules stumbled and only just caught herself. She looked up to see a battle raging around her. The demon wyrms were everywhere. They fought against a band of women who were attached to some big gladiator-looking dudes with chains. There were dragons flying around too. Mostly gold and black ones. They focused their part of the battle against a huge black dragon. Eek. The Black Dragon.

Then she saw a glimpse of one, no, two red dragons.

Dax. He was here. She opened her mouth to call out to him at the same time he spotted her. He folded his wings and dove for her. He was focused solely on her and didn 't see the burst of black flame coming for him.

Jules screamed, but in the din of the battle she couldn't be heard. The black flame hit Dax in the side and he went tumbling toward the floor of the cave and crashed hard into the wall.

"Dax, no, no, no. I'm coming." Jules had never sprinted so fast in her life. She dodged demon wyrms, jumped over spiked dragon tails, and ducked to avoid fire bombs flying over her head. She wasn't the only one who'd seen Dax crash to the ground. A group of demons were scrambling toward his unmoving body to kick him while he was down. She was not going to let that happen. Baseball bat or not, she would defend her mate.

"Jules, thank the moon, help me, please, help me." A woman's voice that was so familiar and yet she'd never heard it before rang through the chamber.

Jules didn't stop running toward Dax, but swiveled her head left and right looking for the woman. Crap. There on a carved bit of stone, raised up from the floor, lay Ellie, fully grown into a young woman. She lifted her arm reaching for Jules but could barely lift it under the heavy chains holding her down.

Jules. Thank the First Dragon.

The sunshine she thought was depleted burst back to life. Dax wasn't dead. She could still be with him, once she explained what had happened and he hopefully forgave her. If those demons didn't get to him.

A baby's screams pierced the air. Behind the rock stood an ancient-looking crone dressed in layers of black tattered robes, holding a crying baby. Jules had seen her before, but almost didn't recognize her without the sticky silver substance all over her face. In her other hand she held a glowing red-hot whip. That woman should definitely not have a baby. Where was the supernatural social services when you needed them?

She didn't know which way to go. Dax was alive, but unmoving and going to be under attack in about ten seconds. But the children were in the clutches of evil and probably about to be tortured. Fear for them all spiked through her hitting her skin like a prickly biting Nor'easter wind.

"Damn it, Jules. Get the necklace to the girl or we're all going to die." Fallyn had a sword in one hand, and pulled daggers from her vest and leggings, tossing them at the demons one by one. She took off heads and arms and legs, turning the onslaught of enemies to sludge in her red-leather clad samurai, crouching demon hidden dragon wake.

And here Jules was sitting around whining like a toddler. She didn't know what to do. Saving the world meant losing the one person who'd become the most important thing in her life. Impossible. She couldn't choose between them and that meant they were all going to die. "I can't."

Fallyn sighed. Middle of fighting literal demons from hell and she sighed. She chopped off the head of the nearest wyrm and stood up, pointing the golden sword directly at Jules. "Get your head out of your ass and use your goddess-given powers, witch. Why do you think I brought you down here?"

"Don't you see? I don't know how. Blowing a little puff of wind isn't going to do a thing to stop everyone from dying. I can't save the world. Even if I am a witch, I'm nothing special ." The goddess had chosen the wrong woman to give the power over the elements too. She wasn't worthy because she couldn't even figure out how to use them or what to do in a serious life or death situation. She should have chosen someone else. Anyone else.

Fallyn yanked the sword back and threw it at Jules. "Use your powers."

There was no mirror this time. When it struck, it was going to kill her. Either that, or hurt truckload. That's what she got for following a morally questionable crazy lady and betraying the love of her life in the process.

The one voice that could make a difference popped back into her head.

You're special to me, lass. You are to a lot of people. I know you don't see that, and that flabbergasts me. But take a look around you. You matter to us all.

A fire started in Jules's chest. She raised her arms over her head and time slowed all around her. The world sparkled with a golden light emanating from her. In the span of a breath, she glanced over to where Dax's body still lay prone on the ground. Up on the raised stone, Ellie reached for her, eyes pleading for help. The baby wailed behind her. In front of Jules, Fallyn's body glowed with a red fire that shined in her eyes and she directed that right at Jules.

From one of the other tunnels a pack of wolves were frozen in mid-air, ready to pour into the fray and fight for everyone's lives. Everyone she cared about was here. Her friends, her family.

They needed her help. They didn't need her.

I need you. Powers or not. I need you for you.

The pure love and sincerity in Dax's words boosted Jules's own confidence in herself like nothing else could. If Dax could believe in her and need her, maybe, just maybe she could believe in herself, too.

She blinked and saw a flash of the immediate future. She knew exactly what to do. She let time catch up with her again and whew, boy did the world erupt around her. Time to take action.

Jules plucked the sword flying toward her out of the air. Not knowing how to handle a storybook weapon, she gripped it like a baseball bat and swung for the fences. The power of wind and sun vibrated inside the sword and Jules used it as an anchor for focusing her powers. Light poured out of her and the sword in huge explosive bursts.

She needed to get herself one of these things. After she saved the world.

The demon dragons surrounding her, the stone where Ellie was, and the ones all over the cave melted in the sunshine she filled the room with like they were the Nazis who looked into the arc of the covenant at the end of *Indiana Jones and the Temple of Doom*. Gross and totally awesome. The gladiator dudes fighting all around her cheered and about half of them shifted into fierce and angry gold dragons.

The remaining ones were still chained, but the women holding their leads were blinded by Jules' light. The men and dragons took advantage of the distraction and either freed themselves or their brethren. A few of the newly freed and shifted threw the women who had been chained to them against the walls or bit their heads off.

Fallyn rushed toward one of the remaining women and blocked any of the dragons from attacking her. "Get back. You can not destroy the Winter Shadow."

The other women rushed to gather behind them and several gold dragons lashed out at the group with rays of sunshine of their own, gusts of gale force winds, talons, and tails. The band of women would have gone down if the attack hadn't been blocked by two huge golds. They landed in front of Fallyn and the women who had just moments ago held them as slaves.

They were going to have to take care of their own problems, Jules still had more work to do. She bolted to her dragon's side and kissed his big ole scales snout. "Dax, babe, are you okay?"

Each place where her lips touched his dragon face, little fires erupted and soaked into his skin. His eyes fluttered open and while they were that of a dragon, she recognized Dax in them too. "Don't you go dying on me, you butthead. I need you too, you know."

Sorry, I was distracted by your utter beauty, that and the fact that you weren't dead. Or allied with evil.

A huge roar filled the cavern, shaking the rock so that pieces of dirt and stone rained down on them from above. Dax extended one of his wings over her head, shielding her from the worst of it. The roar was answered by bellows from at least half a dozen other dragons. Jules peeked out from under Dax's wing and saw the Black Dragon facing down three other ones almost as big as he was. The gold one stood at the front of the pack, the tip of the sword, but was backed up by a red and another black one.

She'd seen all but the other black one in her vision. They all had a certain something special about them and instinct, or maybe her newfound psychic powers, informed her these dragons were the alphas. The ones Dax called Wyverns.

Jules blinked like before and saw another glimpse of the

near future. The Black Dragon would not die this day. He was going kill the three Wyverns with help from that crone. He would get away and take Ellie with him.

Jules blinked again and saw a different future. One where she ran toward the standoff, slipped the necklace over Ellie's head, saving her.

She swallowed down the bile rising up the back of her throat. She could save Ellie and the Wyverns. She would also die by the hands of the Black Dragon if she did.

DARK VERSUS LIGHT

Dax was hurt bad. He was pretty sure one of his wings was broken, along with several ribs, and internal organs. He should be dead. He couldn't care less about his injuries. Jules was alive and well, and whoa was she ever powerful. He'd never even seen Cage wield wind and sun the way Jules had with that sword over her head like a freaking lightsaber.

The force was strong with this one.

Not to mention the way she'd pulled the fire inside of him up to heal his wounds just now. Her love had done that. He had to live. For her.

"Flabbergasted, huh?"

Completely, lass. I will spend the rest of my days proving to you exactly how special you are, if you'll have me. I'm sorry I didn't trust you. I'm a fool. He put on his best Elvis impression, even if his voice was still a bit weak. *But I can't help falling in love with you.*

She nuzzled his snout and in a low husky voice said, "Thank you, thank you very much."

She was so fucking cute. He wanted nothing more than to finish this battle so he could get her home and do lots of dirty things to her. He slowly got up to his feet. He wouldn't shift until the fire in his dragon could heal more of his injuries. Besides, this was the best way to fight, beside her. More than anything he wanted to wrap her up in cotton and protect her from the horrors of hell. No can do. She was born to be a warrior. *Ready to finish this with me?*

Jules bit her lip and if he was in his human form he would have joined her in doing that. "I am, but you're not going to like what I'm about to tell you about how we go about doing this."

The standoff between the Wyverns and the Black Dragon raged on the other side of the room, pulling Dax's attention out of his little bubble of love and life with Jules. The Black Dragon wouldn't let them get any closer to the Black Witch, who was performing some sort of ritual over a baby and the girl.

Go on.

Jules glanced toward the black swirling magic around the children too and lifted her chin, setting her jaw. "I figured out how to control my visions of the future and I've seen two outcomes here. In one we all die."

I vote for the other one then.

She narrowed her eyes at the Black Witch and tightened her fists. "In the other one, we save the world. But ¦ I die."

I choose C. None of the above.

"Yeah, me too. But unless you know where to find a Green Witch and that Blue one who didn't seem to think she was a witch, I'm out of ideas."

Did he know where to find a Green Witch? Of course he did. While half the dragons had been led through the shadow down into this pit of hell underneath the Dragon Tree by Jett, the Demon Dragon Wyvern, Cage, and Match, a contingent had stayed up above with the wolves to battle any stragglers or escaping evil doers.

That contingent happen to consist of his good buddy Steele who was mated to Fleur, the most powerful earth witch around. Plus Jakob and Ciara were up there with Azy. When Kai and Jada arrived from all the way on the other side of the world in New Zealand, they would have all the most powerful Wyverns and witches. Dax had no idea how he ended up in this elite group, but he knew without a doubt that Jules belonged on the team. Where she went, he would follow.

Indeed I do. They're both up on the surface at the Dragon Tree. What's your plan?

"What? Oh. I don't really have one. I just know that we need all the witches and all the dragons to hold off the Black Dragon and Ereshkigal. If we can do that, I can get this to Ellie." She dangled a necklace with a glowing charm in front of his face.

And?

"Umm. I don't know what happens after that. I just know Ellie and Izzy need these necklaces and they and their dragons are the key to defeating the Black Dragon. I haven't tried to see that. Fallyn showed me."

Crazy Fallyn? The one over there defending the succubae who imprisoned the gold dragons?

Jules nodded and bit her lip again. "She's not evil. She's just scared. There's a lot she doesn't know about the world. There's also a lot she does know but it's really confusing and I don't understand most of it. I just know she's on our side."

Okay. I don't trust her farther than I can throw her, but I do trust you. Let's make this happen. I'll call the other dragons down

*and tell them to bring their mates. Then you get with them and do
your thing. Don't die, you hear me?*

Jules reached out touched his face and he pressed into her
hand. "I won't if you won't."

Deal. Ready?

She nodded and Dax mentally broadcasted to the other
dragons. He had no idea of the Black Dragon could hear him
or not, but it wouldn't matter in a minute anyway. Surely he
couldn't sustain his position against an attack of all the
Wyverns and their mates for very long even if he knew they
were coming.

The Black Dragon roared and a whole new batch of
demon wyrms formed in the shadows. The first wave of
them were taken out by the Demon Dragons and the Golds
who had escaped. Still more came. The lull in the battle was
over.

Dax sent up a quick prayer to the First Dragon for
strength and courage and then watched as his mate joined
Fallyn and the succubae. She said something to the group and
Fallyn whooped. That was one strange chick. Match had his
hands full with her.

The ceiling of the cavern opened above them as great roots
reached down from above. The wolves howled in a hair-
raising cacophony and it seemed as if the world was ending.
Not today, it wasn't. Jules and Fallyn threw up some kind of
magical shield over themselves and the falling debris, then as
one moved toward the Black Witch. Dax still couldn't fly, but
he could lay down suppressing fire.

He lumbered forward and shot flames at anything that
moved in the general direction of Jules. He was joined by a
whole host of allies. Jakob, Steele, and Kai slid down from the
ceiling and shifted in midair to their dragon forms. Right

behind them were Azy, Jada, Ciara, and Fleur, who dropped gently to the floor on a big branch.

Jules waved the women over and had soon enveloped them into Team Ladies-Who-Kick-Ass. Their plan was working.

The Black Dragon and Ereshkigal had their backs up against the wall and were being attacked from all sides. Dragons, wolves, and witches were all working together for the win.

The witch bared her teeth and pounded the raised stone block the girl and the baby were on. "If you want this dragon's soul, Kur-Jara, hold them back. I need more time. He's a stubborn brat."

The Black Dragon opened his wings and spread them wide. A darkness blacker than anything Dax had ever seen spread from underneath them. He roared and spewed black fire and smoke into the air above the triple threat army fighting him. The ground beneath them all bubbled and boiled as the blackness spread and the same oily evil rained from the cloud above them. The first of the dragons to be touched by the black roared out in agonizing pain. Their skin burned under the onslaught. Several took to the air, but the dark rain from above pierced holes in their wings and sent them soaring back to the ground.

Dax was far enough away that he wasn't yet touched by this torturous device of the Black Dragon. He was also helpless to do anything for his fellow warriors. He had try anyway. He sent one last plume of fire over the heads of the women and jumped into the rain of fire. He ignored the pain, his broken wing was mostly numb anyway.

A drop of the vile liquid hit him square in the face and it seeped into his skin and penetrated his skull. The darkness in his own soul surged up to protect him. His vision clouded over with blackness and his injuries mattered no more. He knew only death and destruction now. He took to the air, spreading his own wings though one didn't obey his commands and he faltered on his path toward his target.

No matter. He would sacrifice all to kill his enemy. He was joined by another dark one and together they stalked toward the one with a soul blacker than their own. No, it wasn't blacker, it was empty. The absence of light tricked him into thinking the creature had a dark soul. He did not. He was nothing.

The creature clapped its wings together and sent all but he and the other dark one hurtling into the abyss of evil. The abyss ruled by the Goddess of the Underworld. He could do nothing for those poor souls now. He and the other dark one must kill the soulless beast before them. A light, bright as the sun, emerged from behind the beast. The Goddess held a sparkling soul in her grasp.

She must not be allowed to give it to the soulless one, the other dark one whispered to him. *Destroy it. Destroy them all.*

They moved toward the Goddess and the soulless one. Something else caught the attention of the darkness in Dax's soul. A light that crawled out of the abyss. This one golden like the sun. It hurt his eyes to even look toward it, yet he felt salvation with in it.

Wait. Light calls to light.

He and the other dark one paused. The light grew and added more colors. Gold, blue, green, white, red tinged by darkness, and all touched by shadow. The light floated toward the Goddess. She didn't like the light and hurried to stuff it all into a vessel. She clearly didn't understand the power of the soul and it did not fit into her chosen container. Only a shard of it could be contained.

She screamed out as the light got closer, and dropped the soul and the shard, retreating back to her abyss. Good. Now they could concentrate on the soulless one.

The beast roared and reared its ugly head. It dove for the remaining disembodied soul. Dax and the other dark one flew into the battle, fighting with all their might against the unnatural beast. It tore at their flesh and still they fought. The light cried out and sent power to them even though Dax didn't understand how they could afford to spare that surge. The light was not his enemy, but it wasn't his friend either. Light did not ally with dark.

He and the other dark one growled at the light and while it shivered and recoiled, it continued to give over its power to them. So be it. They would use that power to defeat the soulless one.

The bright soul hovered, lost. The golden light darted forward away from its pack and laid a sparkling charm on a smaller dimmer light near the soul. The soul quaked and reached for the sparkling charm. It touched the charm for only the briefest of moments and then sank back into the body it had been ripped from.

That angered the beast and it called forth its dark army. Dax and the other dark one tore through the demons like the nothingness that they were. The beast had nothing to defend it now and no prize to fight for. They could destroy him.

The soulless beast stank with fear and turned to flee into the abyss as well. The light blocked its path but it barreled its way through them, knocking all aside except for the red light tinged with a darkness of her own. Dax was distracted by the distress of the golden light.

He did not care. The golden light reached for him. He did not care about it. Her. Nothing mattered except destroying the beast. Yet the light called to him. His darkness receded. There was light inside of him too.

You betrayed me, little red devil, the beast said to the shining red light. *I protected you from the dragons all those years, and this is how you repay me. You are dead to me, daughter. I will protect you no more. Death to a dragon is your fate now.*

The beast struck out at the red light with its tainted fire and Dax could do nothing. The golden light held him hostage. He could not resist her pull on his soul. The other dark one was not hampered by the light and threw himself at the soulless one. No, not at the beast, but in front of it, between the black fire and the red light.

The fire struck the dark one down and it landed at the feet of the red light. The light did not like that the dark one had sacrificed itself and she exploded, sending the soulless one deep into the abyss. With the Goddess of the Underworld and her minion the soulless one both gone, the light cheered. Others joined in the celebration.

Dax's darkness wasn't quite ready to retreat. It liked the taste of blood in the air and wanted more. He let the darkness bubble back up and spread through him until he was almost fully dark once more. He could destroy all the evil in this place. It would be easy. The wolves hiding at the edge of the cave were not pure of heart. They would be the first to go. The town up by the water was filled with humans and their sins. If he didn't destroy them, the plague of demons would taint them and turn them against the dragons.

"Dax? Look at me."

The golden light, a human, bright as the sun, appeared

before him. He liked her light. He wanted it for himself. Her light, his darkness, together would be unstoppable.

Come to me, light bringer. We will destroy all the evil around us together.

The light inside of her grew and she pushed it toward his chest. It was warm and he liked the feel of it. He moved closer, wanting more of her. She didn't back away as the light had before. A tingle sparked in his chest, one that he decided was caused by her.

Her light poured into him and yet did not lessen her own. "Mm, maybe later. Right now, I'd like you to stop setting the roots of the dragon tree on fire and shift back to your human form too. Can you do that for me?"

Why would I take that weak form when I have all the power we need to destroy our enemies flowing through me now? Perhaps this bright human wasn't what she appeared. He wouldn't believe that. She was something special. Special to him.

She was his.

"Because I'd really like to kiss you," the light said.

Darkness didn't kiss. He was more than darkness though. He was a warrior, a dragon. Dragons didn't kiss. They took, they conquered, they claimed.

Mark. Claim. Mate.

This woman was his mate. The light from inside of her shone through in a mark on her neck and shoulder. She bore his mark. She was his.

And he was hers.

The darkness inside of Dax shrunk until it was nothing more than a small mark on his soul once again. He looked down into the worried face of his mate. Jules. The light of his soul.

He shifted back to his human form and pulled her to him,

squeezing her tight. Her body fit to his so perfectly and he bent her back and kissed her and kissed her and kissed her some more. He only broke the kiss so he could fly them both out of there and to the seclusion of her sunny little bedroom with the fireplace. "You saved me, lass. I've had enough darkness for one day. Let me take you home now and—"

He whispered all the dirty things he wanted to do with her into her ear.

"Wait, Dax. Put me down, we can't leave yet. Your boss is hurt." Jules's scent of ripe peaches and love washed over him, but it was tinged with a smoky sadness. She pointed to a circle of people standing around the hulking form of Match in his dragon form.

They rushed over and pushed their way through the mass of dragon warriors, wolves, succubae, and witches. Match's breathing was labored and black scorch marks marred blistered skin where his scales should be. Jakob, Steele, and Fleur were all treating him with their healing Dragon's Breath. But it didn't seem to help. Fallyn sat on the ground holding his great head, horns and all in her lap, petting his snout.

"Not yet, you big stupid dragon. Not yet." Fallyn reached beneath her leather armor and yanked at the collar and sleeve, tearing it away. There, on her neck and shoulder was the red tattooed mark of a dragon's mate. The crowd around her gasped. She touched two fingers to the mark and cried out. "Mother, help him."

A shining star descended down into the dark pit and landed next to Match. "Are you sure this is what you want, Dragon's Daughter?"

"Yes. Please help him." Tears streamed down her face and onto Match's scales.

"As you wish, but this means he will now be able to find

you. You can't run anymore." The star pulled a red light from Fallyn 's chest and sent it flowing across to Match.

The dragon sucked in a deep breath and his skin knit back together, the scorches healed, and he shifted back into a man before everyone's eyes.

Fallyn bent over him, kissed him on the forehead and whispered, "Not yet."

She reached down to her belt and pulled the mirror and sword from it, held the mirror facing out, and swung the sword over her head.

REVELATIONS

*J*ules blinked, trying to clear the haze from her eyes. The world around her was cool and quiet, like an early spring morning on the weekend before anyone else was awake. Even though the air held a chill, she was warm inside and out. Dax was beside her, holding her hand.

Either she was waking up from a really strange dream, or she'd been abducted by aliens. No. Neither of those was right. They had been fighting a battle. They'd won. Jules blinked again and found herself standing in the clearing, near the Dragon Tree where the wolves had their mating ceremony. A light fog swirled and circled through the trees and around her feet. She glanced around and found groups of other dragon warriors, the Troikas, and a whole coven of succubae including Portia, standing in the clearing with them. A young man and a young woman stood in the middle of them all, holding hands.

She wore a pendant that glowed gold and blue. He wore a talisman with an eerie gray light that encircled them both.

"Ellie, is that you?" Galyna stepped toward the couple, tentatively. Maxsim touched her shoulder and they moved forward together.

"Mom?" The girl dropped the you man's hand and ran toward Galyna.

Cage and Azy ran into the circle. "Apollo. Are you okay?"

The young man's face collapsed into agony and he shook his head. He walked into the waiting arms of his parents who surrounded him in their embraces, hugging him tight.

Jules squeezed Dax's hand. "Weren't we just in a battle? How did we get here?"

"Your guess is as good as mine, lass. The last thing I remember is Match on the verge of death. But he's standing over by that tree looking like his usual cranky-ass self, so I guess whoever saved him, sent us all back up here."

"Fallyn." Jules looked around the gathering of people who milled about together, but didn't see the strange Red Witch anywhere. "But I think she had help from someone else. It's all very fuzzy in my mind."

A very pretty and curvy blonde woman who stood near them walked over. "I agree. This weird lapse in all our memories reeks of the White Witch's doing. She's sneaky like that. I've had all kinds of lost time since I first met her, and I'm still not even sure what she looks like. Yvaine is the only one who's met her and remembers it all. Also, hi. I'm Ciara, the unofficial mates club welcome committee."

Jules took Ciara's hand and shook it. Any residual worry and anxiety she had melted away like snow on a warm day. "Hi. I'm Jules."

Ciara winked at her. "I know. You've met Azy, that's Fleur, Jada is over there talking to her sister Portia, and Yvaine's off galloping through the woods somewhere, I'm sure. So, when's the wedding?"

"*Milacek.*" A man in a deep green shirt and a twinkle in his eye placed a hand on the back of her neck in a very intimate gesture. "They've only been mated for a day, give them a little time before you have their nuptials all planned."

She fake frowned and handed Jules a shiny white card. "Call me. I've got the best cake and flower people."

The man dragged Ciara away, but she shouted over her shoulder, "Welcome to the family. We've all been waiting for Dax to find his redhead."

Jules reached up and tugged on a strand of hair. "I forgot it turned red."

"I didn't. You look flaming hot, my love. Now can we go home? Before we get accosted by any other Wyvern's mates?" Dax went wide-eyed at something behind him. "Too late."

"What the hell did you do to my babies?" Azy stomped over, towing the boy from the clearing and another pretty brown-skinned girl with matching golden eyes behind her. "They were children a few hours ago, and look at them now. Apollo is a handsome young man and my Izzy is not a little girl anymore."

"Oh, you're Izzy?" Jules looked to the pretty young lady. She lifted her chin and nodded. "I have something for you."

Jules reached into the bodice of her dress and found the other package Fallyn had given her. She flipped it open and slid the necklace out into her hand. The charm at the end of the chain swirled in a constantly changing shape inside its golden orb. Jules hung the necklace over Izzy's head and as it settled on her skin, a flash of gold light whooshed across the ground shaking the plants and leaves around them.

On the other side of the clearing, from the center of the

gathering of Troikas a wolf howled and then tore out across the forest.

Ellie shouted after him. "Tristan, wait." Then she too shifted, much more gracefully, without the tearing and rending of muscle, bone and clothes usually associated with wolf shifts. Her small blue-grey wolf ran after Tristan's along the same path.

Two more bigger wolves tore through the men's bodies and clothes as they became beasts and took off after the younger ones. Niko shook his head and glanced over at her. "Fucking dragons." He too shifted, his clothes splitting off of him into tatters on the ground and his body reshaped itself into the largest of all the wolves. He ran out into the forest and his howl ripped through the air.

"Guess I'll go get the in-case-of-emergency-shifting kits from the truck. I'll have to stock up on clothes in Ellie 's and Tristan's new adult sizes. Although Ellie didn't seem to lose hers when she took on her wolf form. Weird." Heli shook her head and trotted toward the reserve's parking area where her truck must be stowed.

Dax tugged on Jules's hand. "This looks like the right break in the action to leave. Let's go home. You're wearing entirely too many clothes."

Jules yanked Dax back before he got more than a step away. She kissed him with the promise of more soon. "Not yet. I think there's more than needs to be figured out before we can go. Just keep your pants on."

"That's easier said than done, lass." He nipped at her ear and for a brief moment Jules considered leaving everyone to their own devices. A new instinct inside of her told her to wait. Something important was about to happen.

Zara, Selena, and Gal headed in the same direction as Heli.

Selena looked at her and waggled her brows. "They grow up so fast."

Azy didn't seem to agree and had missed the other implications of Selena's words. She stamped her foot in the leaves and the ground underneath her turned into a mud puddle. "No, they don't. I'll admit my kidlets were growing at an extraordinary rate, but yesterday, they were toddlers. Cage said yours were babies, Galyna. What in the hell happened?"

Izzy and Apollo exchanged glances and then nodded at each other. Izzy took her mother's hand. "Jules and Fallyn didn't do anything but help us. The transition would have been a lot harder for all four of us if they hadn't been using their powers to guard and protect. We were lucky they could use their psychic abilities to see what was going on. Fallyn beat off the Galla demons more than once during one of our training sessions so that we could learn battle skills from the First Dragon and magic from the White Witch."

The puddle around Azy's feet got even squashier. "Galla demons? The First Dragon? The god-damned White Witch? I'm going to murder them all."

Apollo wiped his hand over his face. "The White Witch and the First Dragon have been preparing us to fight against the Black Dragon. The final uprising from hell is coming and it is our fate to be either sacrifice or savior."

A fountain of water geysered up beneath Azy and as it lifted her above all their heads her legs transformed into a shining golden mermaid tail. "No, you are not. You two are grounded for the rest of your lives, and I forbid you to hang out with those troublemakers ever again."

Water spewed from every which direction and swirled around the twins, encasing them in bubbles of air inside giant pods of water. Izzy folded her arms and rolled her eyes, but she also smiled with obvious affection for her mother and her antics. She mouthed something from inside the bubble that they couldn't hear, but that looked like "Silly mermaid."

"Don't you call me silly, young lady. I am your mother and what I say goes." Azy wagged her finger at the wavery images of her twins through the water. "Apollo, what do you think you're doing? Stop that. Stop that right now."

Gray light shimmered over the young man and great big gold wings burst out either side of the water bubble. He wobbled slightly in the air until Cage shifted too and helped his son up with a gust of wind. The two of them soared into the sky and the water from Apollo's body rained down on them all.

The rest of the Gold Dragon Warriors who had been rescued from hell shifted too and joined Cage and Apollo in the sky. All but two. It looked like they were refereeing a fight between the black-haired woman Ciara had pointed out as Jada and her sister, the succubus from hell, Portia.

Dax stepped right into Jules's view of the argument. "Lass, you're giving me entirely too much time to think up a lot of scintillating tortures for you for making me wait to get you back into bed. This doesn't concern us. Let's go."

"Sweetheart, sugar, honey, sweetie. I promise to do all manner of naughty things to you soon. But in a few minutes. I promise you're going to want to wait for this."

"Wait for what? You naked in front of the roaring fireplace sharing my fire?" Dax licked his lips and his eyes twinkled.

He was hard to resist.

"That too." Jules rubbed a thumb over his jaw and nuzzled against him. She wrapped his arms around hers and twisted so they could both see the result of the disagreement between the two sisters. They didn't know it yet, but their tiff was about to set them both on a path toward finding their true powers too. Not a fun path, especially for Portia, but she'd get her rewards in the end.

Portia said something to Jada that they couldn't hear, but it made Jada ball up her fists and her pearly white skin to go flush. Portia didn't get the hint and kept pushing. She got a slap across the cheek for it.

The two dragon warriors grabbed Portia and yanked her behind them. They formed a wall of muscle between the women, their dragon eyes flared, and horns sprouted out the top of their heads, their dragons preparing for another battle. The darker tattooed man, Jada's mate, jumped in front of her and blue scales shimmered across his body. "Step off, boys. Tempers are flaring and I can't allow any harm to come to my mate."

Dax whispered into Jules's ear. "This is what you wanted me to see? Zon and Gris protecting a succubus? Or was that girl on girl action. You're a dirty bird, aren't you?"

"Shush your face and pay attention, mister. I'll show you just how dirty I am later."

"First Dragon help me," Dax groaned. He held her tighter and it was a good thing she was standing in front of him or the whole group would see the prominent bulge in the front of his pants that was currently poking her in the butt.

Gris got his dragon under control first. "My apologies, Blue Wyvern, but your mate can not be allowed to strike the Succubus Queen."

Jada popped her head out from behind her mate. "Queen?"

Zon filled them all in. "Yes. When I killed Geshtianna, Portia became the highest-ranking succubus. She is the heir apparent, only to be initiated by their maker. You must submit to her rule."

Jada laughed and laughed and laughed. Portia turned and stomped off into the forest. The two warriors scrambled to follow her, practically falling at her feet. It would be interesting to see which, if either, was able to win her cold heart. Jules couldn't quite see that far down their path. There was too many divergences for the outcome to be clear. It would all depend on her figuring out she was worthy of their love.

Which was not an easy task for any woman, Jules included. She almost hadn't allowed herself that happiness. She'd gotten there in the end. Partly because he'd shown her the way.

"I'll admit, that was an interesting revelation. I would have been just as happy to hear that bit of gossip from you. Later. After I'd made you come a couple dozen times. How about we make that happen now, hmm?"

He was nothing of not persistent and she loved him for it. "Just one more thing, lover boy, and then you can take me home to orgasm to your heart 's content."

"Jules, I don't really care what happens in all the other Wyrs. The Reds never have this much drama. It's time to go home." Dax's patience had run out and he picked her up and threw her over his shoulder, rear end in the air.

"Daxton Cervony." The voice of the Red Wyvern rang out.

"There it is. Kindly put me down so you don't get your due with my butt sticking out in everyone's faces."

"Kneel." Match's voice still had that grit to it that only being close to death could give it.

He probably still looked like shit, too. Not that she could see because Dax did kneel, but did not set her down. Jules kicked her feet, to no avail. Dax simply held her tighter.

"My second in command has informed me he too has found his mate and wishes to resign his position. I must choose another. You have proven yourself in battle, and your mate is unafraid to use her powers to fight against the Black Dragon and the evil he sows on our world. I'd like to promote you to the Red Wyr's second. If I fall, you will become the Wyvern in my place."

Dax didn't say anything. So Jules poked him in the ribs. "Say yes and thank you. I've already seen that you're going to be a great leader. You're going to get everyone baseball bats and teach them how to lop demon wyrms heads off with them. It'll be fun."

Dax bowed his head. "Thank you, Wyvern. I accept."

"Good. Then rise with your new mantle of responsibility on your shoulders."

Dax stood and shook hands with Match. "What's my first assignment, sir?"

Jules couldn't be sure because she was still staring at Dax's cute butt, but she thought she heard Match chuckle. "The first thing you need to do is take your mate home and bed her, son. I think you've made her wait long enough."

Dax didn't wait another second before he had Jules cradled in his claw in they were whizzing through the air toward her house and he filled her head with all the things he couldn't wait to do with her when they got home.

"You're a dirty, dirty dragon, my love."

***

Not quite ready for Jules and Dax's story to be over?

Sign up for the Curvy Connection list and get a sexy times epilogue for them!

Plus you'll be the first to know when the new Alpha Wolves Want Curves series comes out. The stories of the Troika wolf-shifters and their mates are coming soon.

YAS! Send me the epilogue and get me on the Curvy Connection now! Sign up here —> http://eepurl.com/ggjqEr

. . .

NEW to the Dragons Love Curves series?

Find the whole series (available in Kindle Unlimited here
—> geni.us/DragonsLoveCurves

ALL CAUGHT up on the dragons and want more shifters?

Check out the bear-shifters in Fated for Curves available at all major online bookstores here —> geni.us/FatedForCurves

WHO LOVES DRAGONS?

A letter from the Author

Dear reader,

I hope you loved reading this adventure in the Dragons Love Curves series with Dax and Jules as much as I loved writing it!

This book is part of the Breath of Air collection. You can get lots more paranormal romances in the collection from a group of today's top romance authors.

Check out all the books here —> http://breathofaircollection.com

The dragons and their mates have a lot more adventures coming your way. But so do the wolves of Rogue, New York.

Yep, the Troika's are all getting their very own books this summer, so if you're into wolf-shifter romance, be sure to subscribe to my Curvy Connection list so you're the first to find out when they Alpha Wolves Want Curves series is available.

I've got some fun surprises coming in the next books in

the Dragons Love Curves series, so be sure to follow me on Amazon, Bookbub, Facebook, or my Curvy Connection to find out what happens next (hint: a certain succubus is going to put up quite the fight when her mates come to claim her.)

Stay tuned to get your fix of sexy dragon shifters giving their mates happy ever afters (and happy endings! Lol)

If you haven't read the book that started it all, check out *Chase Me* where you'll get to read about Jakob Zeleny, the Green Dragon Wyvern, and his mate Ciara's love adventure. You can binge read dragon shifters and their curvy mates for days!

I'd love if you left a review for this story. I really appreciate you telling other readers what you thought.

Even if you're not sure what to say – it can be as simple as – "Loved this story." or "Hooray for curvy girls and dragons." Just one sentence will do a lot.

Want to be the first to know when the next book comes out (plus get cool exclusive content from me!)? Sign up for my Curvy Connection mailing list. Go here http://geni.us/GiveMeCurvyConnection

Find me at www.AidyAward.com or on Facebook, Twitter, Instagram, or follow me on BookBub.

Kisses,

~Aidy

The Curvy Love Series

Curvy Diversion

Curvy Temptation

Curvy Persuasion

Curvy Domination (coming soon)

The Curvy Seduction Saga

Rebound

Rebellion

Reignite

Dragons Love Curves

Chase Me

Tease Me

Bite Me

Cage Me

Baby Me

Defy Me

Dirty Dragon

More dragons coming soon!

Fated for Curves/ Magic, New Mexico

A Touch of Fate

A Tangled Fate

A Twist of Fate

More Space Rangers coming soon!

ABOUT THE AUTHOR

Aidy Award is a curvy girl who kind of has a thing for stormtroopers. She's also the author of the popular Curvy Love series and the hot new Dragons Love Curves series. She writes curvy girl erotic romance, about real love, and dirty fun, with happy ever afters because every woman deserves great sex and even better romance, no matter her size, shape, or what the scale says.

Read the delicious tales of hot heroes and curvy heroines come to life under the covers and between the pages of Aidy's books. Then let her know because she really does want to hear from her readers.

Connect with Aidy on her website. www.AidyAward.com get her Curvy Connection, and join her Facebook Group - Aidy's Amazeballs.

20823473R00116

Printed in Great Britain
by Amazon